FROM THE
NANCY DREW FILES

THE CASE: Stop gossip columnist Beverly Bishop from publishing her latest exposé.

CONTACT: Senator Marilyn Kilpatrick, Nancy's long-time friend whose career is at stake.

SUSPECTS: Della Hawks—the young and beautiful wife of old Justice Hawks. What does Beverly know that could hurt her?

Jillian Riley—Beverly's archrival, who writes the gossip column for the competing newspaper. Is she ambitious enough to sabotage Beverly?

Senator Marilyn Kilpatrick—loyal friend of Nancy and Carson Drew. She has a firm reputation for honesty. Is she hiding something from her past?

Matt Layton—handsome war hero. He aims to win Senator Kilpatrick's seat—at any cost.

COMPLICATIONS: If Beverly Bishop reveals Senator Kilpatrick's secret, tennis pro Teresa Montenegro's life will be in danger. And Nancy is almost her exact double.

Books in THE NANCY DREW FILES® Series

Available from ARCHWAY paperbacks

THE NANCY DREW FILES™ CASE·29

PURE POISON

Carolyn Keene

AN ARCHWAY PAPERBACK
Published by POCKET BOOKS
New York London Toronto Sydney Tokyo

AN ARCHWAY PAPERBACK *Original*

An Archway Paperback published by
POCKET BOOKS, a division of Simon & Schuster Inc.
1230 Avenue of the Americas, New York, NY 10020

ISBN: 0-671-64696-6

First Archway Paperback printing November 1988

10 9 8 7 6 5 4 3 2 1

Printed in the U.S.A.

IL 7+

Chapter

One

Nancy! It's Senator Kilpatrick in Washington, for you!"

Eighteen-year-old Nancy Drew took the phone from her father, an expectant look on her pretty face. "Nancy Drew speaking," she said in a pleasant, self-confident tone.

"Please hold for the senator, Ms. Drew," said the senator's secretary.

Carson Drew pointed in the direction of the kitchen. "I'll get us some tea," he mouthed while Nancy waited for the senator's staff member to put the call through.

Senator Marilyn Kilpatrick had been an old friend and legal client of Carson Drew's since

Nancy was a little girl. The last time the senator had asked to speak only to her, she had led Nancy to a dangerous case that turned out to be a matter of international intrigue. Was it possible that something just as urgent had come up again? Nancy wondered.

"Hello, Nancy." Marilyn Kilpatrick's rich voice floated over the wires. "How's life in River Heights?"

"Fine," answered Nancy with a smile. "But we miss you on the city council."

Marilyn Kilpatrick had started her political career in River Heights. Her work in Nancy's hometown earned her the kind of public trust that eventually got her elected to the United States Senate.

"I miss those days sometimes, Nancy. Washington can be tough."

Nancy frowned. There was a hint of anxiety in the older woman's normally vibrant voice. "Is something the matter, Senator?" she asked. "You sound upset."

Marilyn Kilpatrick hesitated. "I do have a problem, Nancy, but I'd rather not talk about it on the phone. Would it be possible for you to come to Washington?"

Nancy's blue eyes widened. If something big was up, she wanted to do all she could for her family friend. She wasn't investigating any mysteries in town, so a trip to Washington sounded exciting, even though she knew it might prove dangerous. "When would you want me to be there?"

"As soon as possible. Take the next available flight out of Chicago. You'll probably get here late, so I'll have my staff book you into the airport motel," the senator said. "I know it's awfully short notice, but this is very important, Nancy. It may be a matter of life and death."

"I'm on my way," said Nancy decisively. "Where and when should we meet?"

"How about my office, first thing tomorrow morning. And Nancy? Thanks. It means a lot—and not just to me. Say hello to your father for me, and tell him not to worry. I'll take good care of you while you're here."

"All right, I'll do that. Take care, Senator. I'll see you soon!"

After she hung up, Nancy leaned back on the sofa in the Drews' living room. "Not just to me"—Nancy recalled Marilyn Kilpatrick's words. Who else did the senator have in mind?

The last time she had worked for Marilyn Kilpatrick, the case had revolved around Teresa Montenegro, a young tennis star from San Carlos who looked almost like Nancy's twin.

Nancy and her friends George Fayne and Bess Marvin had saved Teresa from an untimely death at the hands of vicious San Carlos assassination squads. Nancy's heart beat a little faster when she remembered how close she had come to getting killed during that case. The memory of it was still very fresh in her mind. She loved the thrill of tracking down criminals, but dodging international death squads was not her idea of a good time.

Carson Drew came back into the living room at that moment carrying two cups of steaming tea. "Well," he said brightly, "and what did Marilyn have to say? Don't tell me she wants you to play sitting target again, because if she does, forget it. You take enough chances in a *normal* day's work."

"Actually, Dad," said Nancy, hunching forward and brushing a hand through her silky reddish blond hair, "she wouldn't tell me what she wanted. She just asked me to come to Washington to find out."

"Oh?" said Carson thoughtfully. "And when does she want you there?"

"Right away," answered Nancy. "She said hello and told me to tell *you* not to worry. So is it all right with you if I start packing?"

"Hmm," her father said, taking a sip of tea. "You're not going to try to catch a plane now, are you?"

"Marilyn wants me to be at her office first thing in the morning," Nancy explained. "I have to take the next flight. I'll stay at a motel near the airport tonight. I'll just take a small suitcase, since I don't know how long I'll be gone. If I need more things, I'll ask Hannah to send them on."

Hannah Gruen, the Drews' housekeeper, had

taken care of Nancy since Nancy's mother had died when she was just three. Hannah had been her nanny, her teacher, her friend—as close to a mother as Nancy could have hoped to have. Neither Carson nor Nancy could have run the household without her.

"Well, I suppose you've got to hear Marilyn out, at least," muttered Carson. "But if this turns out to be another death squad case, I want you to turn right around and come home!"

"Okay. I promise," Nancy said as she stood up, anxious to get ready. It would only alarm her father if she mentioned that Marilyn had termed it "a matter of life and death." He was worried enough about her already. Nancy knew it wasn't easy for him to have a daughter who was always getting into dangerous situations, and Carson bore it about as gracefully as any father could have.

"I'll be fine, Dad," she assured him, kissing him on the cheek. "I'll call you at the office tomorrow, okay?"

"Don't forget," he said, giving her a quick hug. "And, Nancy, watch your step in Washington. Remember, you're my only daughter!"

"The senator will be right with you, Ms. Drew," said the young man at the desk, giving Nancy a more than polite smile. Guys usually found it hard to ignore Nancy's good looks, and this one was no exception.

5

Even though she liked the attention, Nancy was loyal to one guy only—Ned Nickerson. Ned had been her boyfriend for a long time, and Nancy doubted that there was a better one in the world. He was loyal and loving, and he had a great sense of humor. Of course, his good looks didn't hurt, either.

Even though they were apart right now—Ned was at Emerson College, while she remained at home in River Heights—their relationship was very much alive. With a polite nod, Nancy sat down in a corner with a magazine.

About thirty seconds later Marilyn Kilpatrick swept out of her office, purse in hand. "Nancy, it's so good to see you!" she exclaimed, giving her a quick peck on the cheek.

"Hello, Senator. How are you?" Nancy asked. She gave the senator an affectionate hug.

"I'm fine, just fine. And remember—it's just Marilyn, please." Nancy nodded. "Let's get going!" Senator Kilpatrick took Nancy's arm and steered her to the elevator.

"Please cancel all my appointments for this morning, Richard," Marilyn called out to the young man. "If anybody phones, I'll get back to them later."

"Right," said Richard with a little wave. "'Bye, Ms. Drew," he called after Nancy. "See you again, I hope." Nancy turned and saw that he was still smiling as she stepped into the elevator.

"Where are we going?" she asked a few minutes later as they headed out into the street.

"Just for a little walk," answered Marilyn Kilpatrick evenly. The senator was a handsome woman, tall and businesslike. Her rich auburn hair had only a touch of gray sprinkled through it, and her large brown eyes sparkled with an unbeatable combination of intelligence and warmth. But that day Nancy saw only how deeply troubled they looked.

Nancy followed along quietly, letting the senator lead the way. When they passed under some shady sycamores, Senator Kilpatrick stopped, pulled out a makeup case, and pretended to give her face a once-over. Then, closing the compact, she turned to Nancy. "It's okay. We're not being followed," she said, relaxing for the first time since Nancy had met her that day.

"Thank you for seeing me, Nancy. I apologize for being so mysterious. Fact is, I brought you out here because I think my office—and my phone lines—may be bugged."

Nancy couldn't believe it. Bugging the office of a United States senator was serious. "What makes you think so?" she asked quietly.

Marilyn threw her arm around Nancy's shoulders as they walked down the sidewalk. "Let me start at the beginning. Have you ever heard of Beverly Bishop?"

"You mean the columnist? I don't usually read

her, but I know about her. I've seen her face on several magazine covers lately. What's going on?"

"Well, she's about to publish her first book. She's promising to 'tell all,' and if you know Beverly Bishop . . ." The senator rolled her eyes and threw Nancy a meaningful look.

Nancy paused and waited for some people to pass them. She wanted to ask her next question in complete privacy. "Marilyn," she said, meeting the senator's eyes, "are you saying Beverly Bishop has something on *you?*"

Marilyn returned Nancy's serious look. "I ran into her at one of Della Hawks's parties the other night. You must have heard of Della—she's a legend here in Washington, married to Justice Hawks. Anyway, Beverly was glaring at me. She's never really forgiven me for not giving her an exclusive interview when I first came to town, so I figured she was just expressing her disdain for me in general. But then she walked up to me and said, 'Be prepared, Senator—the whole world is soon going to know your intriguing little secret.'"

Marilyn gave a little shiver as they started walking back toward the Senate building. Nancy watched the worry lines in the senator's forehead reappear. The implication was clear. Marilyn Kilpatrick had a secret—a big one.

"All right," continued the senator, almost whispering. "I know what your next question will be, so here's the answer. I suspect that Beverly Bishop has found out that I did something illegal to get Teresa Montenegro out of San Carlos."

So it *was* about Teresa again!

"And it has occurred to me that Beverly might have hired someone to tap my phone," the senator continued. "I want you to know, Nancy, that my personal life is clean. I knew a long time ago that I wanted to work in government, and I've always acted accordingly. And as far as my political past is concerned, integrity has always been my watchword.

"San Carlos was in the middle of a civil war. At the time, Teresa's entire family was dead or in prison, and there was no one to help her—no one to stop her from being killed.

"Maybe I shouldn't have done it, Nancy, but I used some of my own money to buy Teresa's safety. I hated making a deal like that, but I couldn't bear to see anything happen to a beautiful, intelligent, and talented girl like Teresa.

"Of course, if it ever came out that I bribed anyone, no matter how good the reason, my career could be ruined.

"Unfortunately," Marilyn went on, walking into the Senate lobby, "there's even more at stake. You see, in order to get Teresa out of San Carlos, I had to swear that certain facts about the thugs would never come out. The thugs threatened to have Teresa killed if I ever revealed their secrets.

"Believe me, Nancy, the people I dealt with are very powerful. They'd think nothing of murdering Teresa, and I'm terrified for her."

Nancy was wondering why the senator had asked her to come to Washington. There was nothing she could do to stop Beverly Bishop's book from being published. Maybe Marilyn Kilpatrick wanted her to find the bugs in her office —or find out how the information had been leaked to the columnist. Nancy had been concentrating so hard that she hadn't even noticed the large number of reporters who had appeared and were surrounding them in the lobby. "Senator, what about the education bill?" one of them called out.

"I fully support it, and I look forward to voting for it," the senator replied just as the doors of the elevator opened and closed, leaving Nancy and her alone. She gave Nancy a weary smile as she pressed the button for her floor.

"Marilyn, how much does Teresa know about the situation with Beverly Bishop?" asked Nancy as they rode up.

"Not much. I couldn't bring myself to tell her anything about Beverly or about the book. Teresa was hunted for so long, and now she's finally making a new life for herself in the United States. I'd hate to see her terrified again. Her biggest problem lately has been to stay away from the press. I just can't tell her that the press already knows everything about her—or soon will. I've got to persuade Beverly to keep quiet—"

The senator stopped talking as they stepped off the elevator and walked down the hall to her office.

Nancy could understand why the senator wanted Beverly Bishop to keep quiet: the whole situation was a political bombshell, and two people were likely to get hurt, at the very least.

"Everyone's out. Hmm," Senator Kilpatrick observed as the two strolled into her empty outer office. "Well, come on in," she said, opening the door to her office. "I think it would be best if you stayed with me, so I'll give you the keys to my apartment, and—"

As the door swung open, the senator and Nancy stopped dead. There, seated in the senator's chair, her black patent leather pumps resting comfortably on the desktop, sat Beverly Bishop. The look in her eyes was pure poison.

"Hello, Marilyn dear," she spat out in a clipped, angry tone. "Just thought I'd drop by to tell you to enjoy your next few days in office, because they're going to be your last!"

Chapter

Two

"Hello, Beverly. This is quite a surprise," said the senator coolly.

"You can skip the amenities, Senator. I said you're through, and I meant it." Beverly Bishop shot Senator Kilpatrick a withering glare and slowly put her feet down on the floor. She stood and smoothed out her black-and-white houndstooth blazer. Nancy noticed that the jacket complemented her straight black skirt and sheer stockings perfectly.

"When the people of this town find out just how phony your so-called integrity is, I predict you'll be looking for work as a waitress in the Senate lunchroom." With a wicked laugh, the columnist anticipated the full effect of her words on Marilyn Kilpatrick.

The senator didn't give an inch. If she was surprised by the viciousness of Beverly Bishop's sudden attack, she didn't show it. "How can I help you, Beverly?" she asked, a tinge of sarcasm in her voice. "I see you've already made yourself quite comfortable."

"Oh, I get around. That's my business, remember?" the columnist purred. "You'll have to excuse me for not saying hello right away, Teresa." This time she was looking straight at Nancy. "I see you take your little refugee tennis player everywhere," she continued in a condescending tone. "Isn't that noble of you."

Nancy didn't want to respond to the columnist's contemptuous comment without practicing her San Carlos accent first. She had to let Ms. Bishop think she *was* Teresa Montenegro, or she'd never get a chance to talk to her later! Fortunately, Beverly Bishop didn't wait for her to speak.

"I just want you to know, Senator," she continued, her voice dripping with venom, "that threats will not work on me!"

The senator looked genuinely confused. "What are you talking about? What threats?"

The columnist pushed a paper across Marilyn Kilpatrick's desk. "'What threats?' How cute."

Pasted on the sheet of plain white typing paper were block letters, which had been cut from magazines. "If you publish, you'll perish," the message read.

"I've been threatened before, Senator, by people who have since plunged into total obscurity. Don't think something like this will stand in my way."

Nancy couldn't help noticing that the senator's fingers shook as she picked up the message. Did that mean that Marilyn Kilpatrick had had something to do with the threatening letter? Nancy wondered. No, that was ridiculous, she assured herself—wasn't it?

"If you think I had anything to do with this—" Marilyn began.

Ms. Bishop cut the senator off with a laugh. "There's no *if* about it, my dear Marilyn. Smell the paper!"

As she lifted the paper to her nose, Marilyn paled. Even Nancy caught a whiff of the cologne the note was drenched in.

"Worth perfume. You've been wearing it for years now—correct me if I'm wrong." Beverly Bishop stood up and walked around the desk. "I hate cheap tricks, Senator. Try this or anything like this again and I'll go straight to the police!"

With that, and a nod to Nancy, Beverly Bishop swept past them toward the door. "Oh," she added, turning around. "Miss Montenegro, please understand that my feelings for Senator Kilpatrick have nothing whatsoever to do with you. In fact, if you ever care to give an interview

—an exclusive, that is—just give me a call."
And, giving an imperious shake of her platinum
blond head, she stepped out of the room and
pulled the door firmly shut.

"Whew." Senator Kilpatrick shuddered and
sank into the chair at her desk. "That really is
strange. She's right about the cologne. That's the
kind I usually do wear. But who could have
threatened her like that?"

"Well, it's got to be a frame-up. My guess is it
was sent by somebody who wanted her to trace
the note to *you,*" said Nancy, pulling up a chair
next to the senator's desk. "Any ideas?"

Marilyn Kilpatrick considered and then shook
her head sadly. "I've always worked so hard at
not making enemies. I didn't think I had any who
would stoop to this sort of trick."

"Then let's try it from this angle—who else is
afraid of what Beverly Bishop may know?" asked
Nancy.

"Good Lord, Beverly has single-handedly
ruined lots of careers in Washington—and mar-
riages, too, for that matter. There are so many
people who might try to stop her from publishing
that book . . ." The senator was absentmindedly
fidgeting with the papers on her desk.

Nancy stared at Marilyn Kilpatrick for a few
seconds. She couldn't believe that the senator
would resort to threats of any kind, even in
desperate circumstances.

"Where do we go from here?" Nancy asked.

"I don't know, Nancy," was the senator's reply. "There doesn't seem to be much we *can* do. Beverly's convinced I wrote that note, and now I know she won't delay publication of her book, either for me or for Teresa. As for finding out who really sent her that threat, well, there must be hundreds of possibilities in this town."

"Not really," Nancy countered. "Who else is Beverly writing about? What other Washington officials does she have something on? Have you heard anything? Even if it's gossip, it might help."

The senator looked confused. "But how will finding out who wrote the note help us to stop Beverly from publishing her book?"

"I'm not sure," Nancy answered truthfully. "But the more we know about Beverly's book, the better. Maybe this other person, whoever he or she is, will have something on her. What we've got to do is find out everything we can about Beverly Bishop—what her sources are, who she talks to, and *especially* who else she has the goods on. Once we know that, maybe we can figure out a way to stop her."

"And just how do you mean to find out all this?" Senator Kilpatrick asked.

"Easy," replied Nancy. "Ask another big Washington columnist!"

Marilyn's eyes widened. "That's brilliant. Just brilliant. And I know just the person you'll want to talk to—Jillian Riley of the Washington *Herald*."

"Great. Tell me about her."

"She's Beverly Bishop's archrival—although she seems a lot nicer. She might be willing to tell what she knows." The senator fell silent for a moment before continuing. "Then again, perhaps she'd want something in return. . . ." she mused.

Nancy snapped her fingers and jumped up. "I've got it!" she cried. "Do you think Ms. Riley would like an *exclusive* interview with 'Teresa Montenegro'? I'll pretend to be Teresa tomorrow, and I'll talk to Jillian Riley about Ms. Bishop while I promise her the interview at a later date. Teresa can do the interview if she wants to later on. I'll say I had a falling-out with Ms. Bishop, and that's why I'm giving her the scoop. And that will bring up the subject of Beverly Bishop's nastiness. What do you think?"

Marilyn Kilpatrick's eyes sparkled. "I think I'm glad I asked you to take this case," she said, picking up the telephone to call the *Herald* office.

Three minutes later it was all arranged. Nancy —or rather, Teresa—had an appointment with Jillian Riley for the following day. "And now," said Nancy, getting up to go, "I'd better give myself a crash course in being a tennis star from San Carlos. Luckily, I've had some practice. The hard part is going to be doing my hair and makeup to look like Teresa's without Bess to help me—but I'll manage." She smiled at the senator. "Where's Teresa staying these days?"

"I'll drive you there myself," said the senator, leading Nancy out of the office. "It's only about ten minutes from here. On the way, we can decide what to tell her. I don't want her to be alarmed about any of this. She's got some big matches coming up in a few days, and she's got to be able to concentrate on her game."

On the way to Teresa's, Nancy stopped at a drugstore and bought makeup for her "disguise." She and the senator decided to play it cool. They'd tell Teresa that Nancy was in town for a short visit, and ask if she could stay with Teresa for a night or two. Then Nancy could study her unobtrusively all evening, and be ready for her big interview at the *Herald* the next morning.

Teresa Montenegro lived in an apartment complex not far from downtown Washington, one of those tasteful yet faceless developments featuring garden duplexes and tight security. After what had happened to her in the past year, Teresa valued security above everything—except her freedom.

At the gate, the attendant saw the senate license plate and waved them in. "Teresa's place is right over there," the senator explained, pointing to a garden apartment at the edge of the property near a man-made lake.

Nancy followed her friend to the front door,

which led into a carpeted foyer with four apartment doors opening onto it. "It's right here," said Marilyn, raising her hand to knock on the second door on the left.

But her knuckles never touched the metal. "N-N-Nancy, look!" she gasped, pointing down at the floor.

There, flowing out from beneath Teresa's door, staining the beige carpet dark red, was a spreading pool of blood!

Chapter

Three

"Teresa!" cried Nancy, pounding on the door. There was no sound from inside.

"What if we're too late?" Senator Kilpatrick cried. "What if something awful has happened to Teresa? I'll never forgive myself!"

Nancy bent down to inspect the bright red stain oozing out from under Teresa Montenegro's door. She gingerly touched the substance with one finger, then smeared a drop of it on her other hand. "It's stage blood," she told her friend when she stood up.

"How can you be sure?"

"It's thicker than real blood, and it doesn't dry or turn brown—it just stays the same. See?"

Nancy held her hand up in front of Marilyn's face.

Nancy could tell she and Marilyn were thinking the same thing. Teresa Montenegro was not a theatrical person. If there was stage blood in her apartment, someone else had put it there.

Stepping back, Nancy pulled her lock-picking kit out of her purse and quickly worked open the apartment door.

Nancy burst into the room with the senator right behind her. The place had been ripped apart. Teresa's tennis clothes were everywhere, most of them slashed. Her furniture was toppled over and several of her tennis rackets had been smashed. Stage blood had been thrown everywhere.

But worst of all were the words scrawled in the fake blood on the living room wall: "Silence or Death."

"'Silence or death,'" Nancy whispered. "'If you publish, you'll perish.'" She looked over at Senator Kilpatrick, who seemed to be in a state of shock. "Any idea who's behind this?" she asked.

"I'd say our dear old friends in San Carlos are trying to send us a little message, special delivery. They must know about Beverly's book, too." The senator found a clean spot on the sofa and sat down with a loud sigh.

"I don't think I understand," murmured Nancy, pacing around the room, taking in the whole grisly sight yet again. "How could these people have found out about what's going to be in Beverly's book? They're thousands of miles away, aren't they?"

"Ah, but they have their ways of knowing." The senator smiled wearily. "Unfortunately, there's no way to control espionage in this town. There are just too many people working out of embassies, consulates, trade delegations, student exchanges—and not all the spies are foreigners, either."

"We've got to find Teresa right away," Nancy said quickly. "Any idea where she might be?"

"Not the slightest," said Marilyn Kilpatrick with a slight scowl. "We could try the tennis cl—"

She stopped in midsentence, staring at the open doorway. Nancy turned and saw Teresa Montenegro standing in the hall, her eyes wide with fear as she surveyed the damage to her apartment.

Looking at Teresa was almost like looking in a mirror for Nancy. Although they didn't have the exact same shade of reddish gold hair, their blue eyes were identical. Teresa's skin was a little darker than Nancy's peaches-and-cream complexion, but they shared the same lean build, and when Nancy wanted to impersonate Teresa—as she had in the past—it was a cinch. She only hoped it would go as well this time, because the famous tennis player seemed to be in even more danger now.

"Teresa—" Nancy started toward her friend.

Teresa's mouth opened, and a stifled scream came out in response. Then the tennis star's eyes closed, and she collapsed onto the floor!

"Marilyn, quick—get some cold water!" yelled Nancy, taking control.

The senator jumped up from the sofa and ran to the kitchen. When she returned, Nancy took the glass of water from her and sprinkled some on Teresa's face. Then she shook Teresa's shoulders.

"Come on, Teresa, wake up!" the older woman pleaded.

When she did come to, Teresa sat bolt upright and cried, "No! No! They're going to kill me! They're after me!"

The senator grabbed Teresa's arms and looked into her eyes. "It's all right," she said, forcefully. "It's all right, Teresa—somebody was just trying to scare you."

Nancy crouched next to Marilyn. "Give her a minute," she advised.

Sure enough, after a few deep breaths, Teresa was able to respond a little more calmly. "I thought they were through bothering me. What can they want? They've already taken everything."

Then Teresa reached over and squeezed

Nancy's hand. "Nancy," she murmured warmly, "what are you doing here?"

"At the moment? Helping you pack," said Nancy. "You can't stay here tonight."

"Absolutely," Senator Kilpatrick agreed. "I want you to come back to my apartment. I have plenty of room. There's a pull-out couch in my study, and you can stay as long as you like. Nancy's staying with me, too."

"You are?" Teresa's face brightened a little when Nancy nodded.

"Then we'll all be roommates for a while. It'll be fun," said Marilyn Kilpatrick, with as much of a smile as she could manage.

"Thank you, Senator. I don't know what I'd do without your kindness." Wiping a little mascara from her face, Teresa got up and went to the bathroom.

When she was out of earshot, Nancy turned to Marilyn. "If Beverly Bishop's book comes out," she said softly, "Teresa will never be safe again, anywhere."

"I know," Marilyn replied with a worried nod. "We've *got* to stop Beverly, and I don't think we've got much time!"

That evening, seated on the comfortable rose-colored velour club chairs in the den of Senator Kilpatrick's elegant town house apartment, Nancy and Teresa caught up on each other's news. As they talked, Nancy watched Teresa carefully—

every gesture, every bit of body language, every habitual movement. She had lost some of her accent in the past few months, and Nancy was glad. It would make her work easier.

Teresa had a way of touching her fingers to her lips when she was thinking. She tended to throw her head back when she was excited about something. Her smile could be shy, with her head down and her eyes focused off to one side. Those were the details, and Nancy was drinking them in. She'd have to imitate them exactly in her interview with Jillian Riley the next day. Not that she was going to give Jillian an actual interview or anything—she just needed to make her *think* that she was. Nancy hadn't told Teresa what she planned on doing, mainly because Teresa had enough to worry about already. Also, Nancy had a feeling that the less Teresa knew, the better for her—at least for the present.

"I love that braid in your hair," Nancy said to Teresa, leaning toward her to examine it. "Could you show me how you do that?"

"Sure. Want to try it right now?" Teresa tilted her head forward and her hair cascaded down. "You just take this piece here, and twist it— No, come sit on the floor in front of me and I'll braid your hair. Then you'll see how it's done."

Nancy reviewed her plan as Teresa worked on her hair. First, she would get her Teresa Montenegro look together and then she'd go straight to Beverly Bishop's office. She would try to persuade the columnist not to publish what she knew. Of course, Nancy wouldn't be too specific —she didn't want to give Beverly any information she didn't already have. Then she'd go see Jillian Riley and—

"Finished!" Teresa exclaimed. "Go see," she said, pointing at the large mirror over the sofa. They both rose and walked over to examine Nancy's reflection. Looking at the two of them standing side by side, Nancy felt certain she could pass for Teresa *anywhere*—with just a little makeup, which she'd apply early in the morning.

"You like the braid?" asked Teresa.

"I love it. But I think I'll turn in now. It's been a long day." Nancy smiled. "Oh, one more thing, Teresa. Could I borrow a top for tomorrow? Marilyn's housekeeper sent that sweater I had on to the cleaners."

"No problem. Just take whatever you want. My things are in the study."

"Thanks. Well, good night," Nancy called as she went off to the guest room. "Sleep well, Teresa!"

She doubted that Teresa would get much sleep after what had happened that day. And as Nancy lay down and put her head on the soft pillow, she suspected that the senator wouldn't be able to close her eyes, either.

Nancy began to drift off to sleep. But two phrases kept sounding in her mind: "Silence or

death"—"if you publish, you'll perish"—
"silence or death. . . ."

Nancy's travel alarm buzzed at eight o'clock.
Opening one bleary eye, she tried to shake off the
fog in her head. Time to get moving.

With a sigh, Nancy rolled across the bed, stood
up, and rubbed her eyes. After taking a shower,
she carefully applied a temporary rinse to her
hair to darken it a bit. Then she applied an
olive-toned base to her skin, along with the
heavier eye makeup Teresa favored. Wrapping a
robe around her, she walked quietly into the
living room. The sun filtered in through the
vertical blinds in bright stripes, and the room
was just as she'd left it the night before.

"Marilyn?" she called softly in the direction of
the senator's bedroom. There was no reply.

In the kitchen, Nancy found her answer in a
note.

"Nancy—help yourself to breakfast. My
housekeeper comes at ten. Call me! Love, M.K."

Nancy flicked on the gas under a white enamel
kettle. Then she walked back through the living
room to the senator's study. After tapping on the
door as lightly as she could, she peeked inside.

Teresa was sleeping peacefully, all her anxiety
and terror forgotten for the moment.

Without a sound, Nancy made her way across
the room and lifted a lavender sweater from

among Teresa's things. Her own charcoal pants would go perfectly with it.

After lightly walking over the rose carpeting and closing the door quietly, she made her way back to the kitchen. Normally, Nancy started the day with some orange juice. Today, though, she was opting for strong coffee—the kind Teresa drank in the morning—because, for now at least, she had to *be* Teresa Montenegro. And the sooner she started, the more convincing she'd be by the time she walked into Beverly Bishop's office.

Clipping her hair back with the barrette Teresa had put into her hair the night before, Nancy stepped back and regarded herself in the mirror. "Good morning," she murmured, with a hint of a Spanish accent. "My apologies—I have no appointment, but I would like to see Ms. Bishop as soon as possible. I have important information for her."

She could do it. She knew she could. She had to.

"Good morning. My apologies—I have no appointment, but I would like to see Ms. Bishop as soon as possible. I have to speak to her."

"Of course, Ms. Montenegro." Beverly Bishop's secretary, a pleasant-looking woman of about fifty, seemed convinced that she was talking to the famous tennis player and not to Nancy Drew, the famous detective. "May I say I admired you tremendously in your last matches. I play tennis myself, and how you can do what you do is beyond me—"

Nancy strained to see through the frosted-glass door into Beverly Bishop's office and could make out two women in there. She couldn't hear what they were saying, but she could tell that one of them was Beverly. The other woman had a high-pitched voice, laced liberally throughout with a southern accent.

"But *why* must you bring this out in the open?" she heard the southern woman saying. "It won't help anyone, but it will hurt me a great deal. Please, don't!"

Nancy didn't get a chance to hear Beverly's answer.

"How did you master that fabulous backhand?" the secretary asked eagerly.

"Lots of practice. If you'll excuse me, I think I'll sit down for a moment and look at today's paper," Nancy said, backing away from the secretary's desk. Whatever was going on in Beverly Bishop's office was too interesting to miss! She took a seat on a small couch and picked up the Washington *Courier*. Pretending to read the day's news, Nancy tuned back in to Beverly's conversation.

"This is a free country, that's why!" Beverly was saying.

"But it will ruin my life! Don't you understand? And it will ruin other lives, too!" The woman sounded even more desperate now. Her voice was becoming louder and higher, and her accent kept moving farther and farther south.

"Well, you should have thought of that before, dear," came the columnist's acid reply. "After all, you can't deny it's the absolute truth."

The door to the office suddenly swung open, and a woman swept out like a gale. Her raven hair fell to just below her shoulders, and her exquisitely beautiful face was washed with tears of frustration. At the secretary's desk, she stopped and turned around to give Beverly a parting comment.

"You witch!" she snarled. Rage filled her perfect gray eyes. "You think you can play with people's lives? Well, you're going after the wrong person this time. If you destroy me, I'll kill you! Don't think I won't!"

Chapter

Four

Nancy stared after the beautiful raven-haired woman as she hurried out of the office. Who was she and what did Beverly Bishop know about her? Nancy knew she'd seen that face before somewhere.

"Oh, dear," the secretary muttered, trying to be light for her guest's sake. "You know, in Beverly's business, feelings run high. Don't worry, Miss Montenegro. Mrs. Hawks didn't mean what she said. Nobody's going to get killed around here."

Hawks—wasn't that the name of the person who'd thrown a party both the senator and the columnist had attended? Nancy wondered. Had Beverly Bishop told Della Hawks the same thing she'd told the senator—that soon the whole world would know her secret?

Just then Beverly Bishop stepped out from behind her desk and marched purposefully to the open doorway. "It's only a book, for heaven's sake!" Her haughty scowl changed to a satisfied smile when she saw Nancy. "Well, well—Teresa! How nice to see you! And to what do I owe the pleasure of this visit? You know I'd love to do a piece on you. Why don't you come in, and we can talk."

Nancy followed the columnist into her office and sat down, crossing her legs just as she had seen Teresa do the night before. She had to remember every last detail of her impersonation, because if anyone would notice, it was Beverly Bishop, whose job was to study people. And the blond columnist would be furious if she ever discovered she'd been fooled! "If you have information about me, I beg you to keep it confidential, Ms. Bishop," Nancy began. "My life has been threatened—"

"My dear, as you know, I've been threatened lately, too. Why, if I had a hundred dollars for everyone who wanted to get rid of me, I'd be a millionaire!" Beverly Bishop interrupted with a facile smile. "You see, it's the American way, Teresa. Free speech, you know. But then, you should appreciate that more than most people.

You wouldn't want the old U.S. of A. to become another San Carlos, would you?"

"Well, no, of course not, but—"

"Besides, if I do a favor for you, I'll have to do one for everybody, now, won't I?" Beverly Bishop was obviously enjoying herself as she turned the screws tighter.

"Don't worry! After all, *you* had no idea what was going on behind the scenes, and I know that. You're going to *love* my new book. Of course, a certain American senator may suffer a bit, but that's life, my dear."

"M-maybe if you tell me exactly what you'll be wr-writing—" Nancy stammered.

"Huh-uh," scolded Beverly Bishop, shaking a finger at Nancy. "You'll have to buy the book just like everybody else."

Nancy nodded, but inside she was furious with the columnist. Della Hawks was right: Beverly Bishop did play with people's lives. She had no concern for the lives she was about to ruin—or end.

"It won't be long, though. The book should be out soon! I've saved the best for last. The remaining chapters are devoted entirely to what I call the big four—people in high places, like your friend the senator. I've completed my work on three so far—two already typed out, the other right over there in that Dictaphone, almost done. Number four is in here." Beverly tapped a dark red fingernail against the side of her head. "It's

33

too significant to let out until the last possible minute."

"I see," said Nancy, trying to sound impressed. She was beginning to understand why Beverly Bishop had so many enemies. The woman was a viper!

Maybe if she found out a little about the process of publishing Beverly's book she'd have a better shot at halting it. "I'm curious. How long does it take to print a book?" Nancy asked.

The columnist took a mirror out of her top drawer and quickly checked her appearance as if it were more important than her book. "Usually they take months to produce, but, Teresa darling, this is a Beverly Bishop book. My publishers are planning on getting it into every bookstore in the nation within three weeks. In fact, I'm sending three chapters in today so that they can start the typesetting. No one dares to edit my books; they are published exactly as I write them. It'll be all set to go—except for that all-important final chapter," said the columnist, smiling like the cat with the canary still warm in its stomach.

She stared at Nancy as if she were trying out a few lines about how to describe Teresa if she ever did a story on her. "Now, I understand it may be a little too soon for you to tell me about your escape from San Carlos and so on, but if you have *anything* you'd like to tell me . . ."

Nancy touched her fingers to her mouth and tilted her head to one side, just the way Teresa had done when she was thinking the night before. "I value my privacy very much. I do not wish to advertise myself or anything like that. I have nothing to tell you."

"Well, suit yourself," Beverly said in an irritated tone. "If you change your mind, come back. And now, if you'll excuse me, I really must get back to work."

With a grand wave of her hand, the columnist dismissed Nancy.

A surge of distaste ran through Nancy, and she felt relieved as soon as she stepped out into the balmy Washington weather. Her appointment with Jillian Riley wasn't until late that afternoon, and Nancy decided to walk and think for a while. The task of keeping Beverly Bishop's book out of print weighed heavily on her mind.

"My apologies—I am a bit early for my appointment, but I hope that Ms. Riley will see me as soon as possible. Please tell her Teresa Montenegro is here, and that what I have to say is very important."

Behind the receptionist's desk, partitioned by glass, the Washington *Herald* offices hummed and beeped like an electronic beehive. Seated at word processors, writers keyed in data from around the globe, while layout artists cut and pasted in a score of cubicles around the huge offices.

"I'll let her know right away. Oh, and may I

please have your autograph, Ms. Montenegro? It's for my little niece. She just loves to watch you play." Nancy bent down to sign the paper the secretary was offering her. So far, so good, she thought. She had practiced scrawling Teresa's signature that morning, copying it from the big signed photograph of Teresa that hung in Marilyn Kilpatrick's home.

Beyond the glass partition, Nancy saw a stylish blond woman about forty years old hang up the phone and look up. Instantly, the woman spotted her through the glass and flashed a smile. But Nancy's experience with one particular columnist had taught her not to trust that professional friendliness.

"You may go in, Ms. Montenegro," Jillian Riley's secretary told Nancy.

"Thank you," said Nancy. She walked into the spacious, well-designed office. "Good morning."

"Good morning to *you*, Ms. Montenegro. My goodness, you've been busy this morning."

Nancy tilted her head quizzically. "Oh?"

"You've already spoken with Beverly Bishop. You must have something terribly juicy to say if you came to *both* of us!"

"But how did you know—" Nancy hadn't anticipated this problem. She had heard about how quickly things got around on the Washington grapevine, but this was ridiculous! Actually, though, this would just make Teresa's story of a disagreement with Beverly more believable.

"Oh, I may not be a genius, but I *do* know everything that goes on in this town," Jillian Riley said arrogantly. "I have to, it's my business!" The columnist laughed. It was an infectious laugh, wicked like Beverly's but somehow nicer. And Nancy, though she was a little shocked by what the columnist had told her so offhandedly, found herself smiling.

"So what can I do for you?" asked Jillian. "I hear you have information for me. What's it about? And is it the same stuff you gave 'dear' Beverly?"

Nancy found herself caught off-balance by the clever shift in conversation. Jillian Riley knew how to make people talk, no doubt about it.

"I went to Ms. Bishop to ask for a favor," Nancy explained. "I asked her please not to say anything about me and my past in the book that she is writing. But she said she would put it in the book, anyway," she whispered, then burst into convincing tears.

"I understand." The columnist nodded. Nancy could almost see her drawing conclusions at supersonic speed. "And you've come to me because . . . ?"

"Because I want the truth to come out!" Nancy said hotly. "Because Teresa Montenegro is not what the book will say she is!"

"And you want *me* to print the truth. Well." Jillian Riley smiled, picking up a pencil and a pad. "Fire away. I'm all ears."

Nancy had expected that Ms. Riley would want the exclusive interview right away, since Teresa had never given one. "No, I cannot say yet. You must wait until after the book comes out."

"But, Ms. Montenegro—Teresa, if I may—the truth will be ever so much more effective if it comes out *before* the lies!"

She was clever, Jillian Riley. Nancy had to admire the way she worked. "I'm so sorry." She shrugged. "There are reasons—other reasons I cannot tell you yet. But you will be there when I am ready, yes?"

"Of course!" said Jillian, putting down the pad and pencil. "So tell me," she urged, "did Beverly happen to mention anything else about her book? Just between us."

Of course. Jillian wasn't all that different from Beverly—they were rivals. Nancy could feel the alligator's mouth opening slowly, ready to devour the least little tidbit of information.

But in this case, Nancy was also looking for information. Finding the truth was *her* job, too! And she had one big advantage over the other woman—Jillian Riley didn't know who Nancy really was.

"She told me she was almost finished with the book, that she was writing about the big four, she called them."

"Aha, the big four, eh?" asked Jillian Riley,

leaning forward in her chair to get a better look at Nancy. "And who might they be?"

"But I thought you already knew everything," Nancy shot back with a sly smile.

"Touché, Teresa. I see you've got wit as well as athletic talent. Yes, I have a fair idea about who the big four might be. Or two of them, anyway," admitted the columnist.

"Oh? Who are they, if you do not mind my asking?"

"No, I don't mind, as long as you give me your story in exchange. I'd say Della Hawks would be one of them."

Della Hawks, the young woman who'd threatened to kill Beverly earlier that morning.

"And, of course, Marilyn Kilpatrick's *got* to be another. Beverly has been trying for years to get something on her. You know it'd be great copy— people would love to read that the first female senator from Illinois got where she is immorally, or illegally."

Nancy suddenly had a flash of insight. "What about you, Ms. Riley? Could you be one of the four she's trying to get? You are Beverly Bishop's biggest rival, correct?"

Jillian let out another infectious laugh. "'Rival' is putting it mildly. Beverly and I can't *stand* each other, although we are very polite to each other whenever we meet. I'd like to cut her throat, and I'm sure she'd love to return the favor. So I might very well be one of the big four. Tell you what, though. If I am, Beverly had better watch out. I've got one or two little weapons of my own."

Nancy was silent for a moment. "And number four?"

"I don't know." Jillian leaned back in her chair and sighed. "But enough about Beverly. I'd rather talk about you. What was it like, really? Your escape to America? Your father being killed? It must have been very hard on you—"

"I am so sorry. These are things I don't care to make public," Nancy said decisively.

The columnist shrugged. "Well, I hate to break this up," she said with a glance at her watch, "but I've got to be off. I've got an interview with the most gorgeous congressman in town—Matt Layton. I don't want to keep *him* waiting."

Matt Layton was the congressman from Nancy's home district. He was known as much for his handsome, rugged looks and charisma as for his heroism in the Vietnam War. Nancy could understand why Ms. Riley was excited about talking to him.

"Here's a little piece of dirt for you." Jillian Riley winked as she ushered Nancy out of the office. "Layton's got his eye on Marilyn Kilpatrick's Senate seat! Boy, that sure would split the female vote, huh?" And with another throaty laugh, Jillian waved goodbye as she pointed Nancy in the direction of the elevators. "See you soon, Teresa."

"Yes," Nancy answered, stepping into the hallway. "Goodbye."

Filled with excitement over the new leads she'd turned up, Nancy nearly flew back to the Senate building, and up to Marilyn's office after a quick stop for a security check. Wait till Marilyn heard about everything!

The receptionist was out, so Nancy went right in to the inner office, not thinking to knock. The senator was staring out the window, her back to the door.

"Marilyn!" she called out.

The senator gasped when she heard Nancy's voice. Wheeling around, her eyes wide in surprise, she held her arms out, and Nancy froze in utter shock.

Marilyn Kilpatrick was holding a revolver— and it was pointed straight at Nancy's heart!

Chapter

Five

TERESA?" MARILYN LOWERED the gun and fell into the leather armchair beside her desk. "I'm so sorry. This whole nasty business is making me a nervous wreck."

"I guess I should have knocked," said Nancy, as lightheartedly as she could manage.

"Nancy, it's *you!* My goodness, you almost had *me* convinced you were Teresa." The senator laughed, releasing some of the tension that had obviously been building up inside her. "You come all the way from River Heights to help me out, and I stick a gun in your face!"

"It's okay, Marilyn," said Nancy. "What are you doing with the gun, anyway?"

Marilyn fingered it, embarrassed. "I just got this for Teresa," she explained. "I hate to say it, Nancy, but I think she does need the extra protection. And when I heard the door open— what can I say?—I panicked. But don't worry. It isn't loaded."

"You have been under a *little* pressure lately," Nancy offered with a sympathetic smile, trying to dismiss the image of Senator Kilpatrick pointing a gun at her.

"Well, how did it go? Tell me everything. Is Beverly going to remove the section about me from her book, for Teresa's sake?"

Nancy pursed her lips and shook her silky hair. "I'm afraid not. In fact, she told me the book's going to be out in less than a month—with a whole section devoted to you."

"Did you tell her that your life was in danger?" The senator's large brown eyes revealed the intensity of her alarm.

Nancy nodded, sighing. "I told her I'd been threatened, Marilyn, but she wouldn't budge."

Marilyn leaned back in her chair. A look of defeat creased her forehead. "How can people be so ruthless, Nancy?"

Nancy shrugged her shoulders. "I guess some people think that tearing other people down will build them up. Look, Marilyn—we're going to keep trying, no matter what. We can still turn this situation around—we have to."

Those words seemed to hit the senator hard.

"You're right," she agreed, straightening up in her chair.

"Now, there's got to be a way for us to intercept the material before it gets to the publisher. That'll buy us a little time, anyway. We need every hour we can get!" exclaimed Nancy.

"But we can't do anything illegal, Nancy. I'm a U.S. senator, remember, sworn to uphold the law."

"I know," Nancy replied. "Believe me, Marilyn, I don't want to get on the wrong side of the law, either."

The senator frowned. "I guess I'll make one last personal appeal to Beverly. If that fails, the only thing we can do is try to ensure Teresa's safety. I'm seriously considering putting her in protective custody, if she wants it. I could call the FBI and get her a whole new identity—change her name and her history. She wouldn't be Teresa Montenegro anymore. She couldn't play tennis, at least not professionally, but at least she'd be alive."

"It would be horrible for her to have to give up tennis!" gasped Nancy. "Teresa's worked so hard to be a champion."

"I know. However, a new identity may be her only hope of being safe." With a sigh, the senator got up and put the gun in her desk drawer.

Nancy felt less nervous, knowing that the revolver wouldn't be going anywhere, at least for the moment.

"Well, I'd better get some of this paperwork off my desk before I go over to Beverly's to make *my* appeal," said Marilyn. "Why don't you head back to my place and keep an eye on Teresa until I arrive? I'll bring home dinner for us all, okay? Do you like Vietnamese food?"

"Never tried it, but I'm sure I'll like it." Nancy stepped toward the elevator. "And, Marilyn—good luck."

The senator threw Nancy a tired smile. "Thanks. I'm going to need it."

"Teresa, you've hardly touched your food."

Nancy, Marilyn Kilpatrick, and Teresa had eaten a late supper in silence. The last-ditch appeal by the senator to Beverly Bishop had failed, so there had been nothing to do but break the news to Teresa. The tennis player was very down on the suggestion that she take a new identity, and Nancy could understand why.

She had never seen her friend so low. Just when she had gotten her life together, just when she thought she had finally put all the fear and pain behind her, everything was crashing down on her all over again.

"Listen, what are we doing moping? We'll think of a way to stop that horrible Beverly!" Nancy said, forcing herself to be positive. "We've still got time."

Teresa nodded weakly, and Marilyn tried to

smile, but the atmosphere in the room remained distinctly heavy.

"In the meantime," said Senator Kilpatrick to Teresa, "until we get out of this mess, I've asked one of my staffers to act as your bodyguard. You know him—in fact, both of you do. Remember Dan Prosky?"

Nancy remembered him, all right. Dan had almost gotten himself killed trying to protect Teresa the last time Nancy was in Washington. Good old Dan—superjock, ex–police officer, loyal, discreet. And Nancy would never forget the death-defying car chase they'd been in together.

"Of course I remember him," Nancy replied happily.

"What an amazing driver." Teresa laughed.

"Does he know about all the trouble Beverly Bishop is causing?" Nancy wanted to know.

Marilyn shook her head. "No, and he doesn't need to—as far as I can see. I've told him Teresa's in danger and it's his job to keep her safe. That's all."

The senator got up. "Oh, and Teresa, I got you something else, too. I know you don't like weapons, but sometimes it's necessary to have one, and I've taken the liberty of getting one for you—with a permit application, of course. The gun is registered in my name for the time being, and you are not to use it or even handle it unless you are in life-threatening danger. You understand, don't you?"

The beautiful tennis player nodded.

"It's in my purse." The senator walked into her bedroom.

"Nancy, this makes me so nervous. I do not like weapons," commented Teresa, twisting her fingers together nervously.

"I know, but it's a good idea to have one here tucked away. Trust me. We might as well put the dishes into the dishwasher," said Nancy. She and Teresa began to clear the table. "Anyway, you won't have to carry it as long as Dan's with you," Nancy reasoned.

Teresa nodded. "I will feel better with Dan here."

Marilyn wandered back into the dining room, her bag in hand. "That's funny," she said, riffling through it, "I was sure I put the revolver in here. Well, I must have left it at the office, then."

"I did see you put it in your desk drawer," Nancy volunteered.

"Right. I thought I took it out later, when I left my office, but I guess I didn't. Anyhow, you two girls'll be okay by yourselves for a little while, won't you? I'll go get it and be right back." The senator took her coat out of the hall closet, and Nancy heard the door shut behind her.

As the two girls loaded the dishwasher, Teresa seemed completely preoccupied.

"I've been thinking about what Marilyn said before, about changing my identity," Teresa said. "Do you think maybe I could be a tennis coach at a school somewhere?" She tried to sound cheerful, but Nancy could tell that she was devastated by the thought of giving up her career.

"Teresa, I know this is hard to believe, but it's going to work out somehow. I'll think of a way to save you and Marilyn, I promise."

But Nancy wasn't absolutely sure that even she could help this time.

An hour later the phone rang. "I'll get it," Nancy told Teresa. They were sitting in the living room, watching TV and trying to relax. "Hello, Senator Kilpatrick's residence," she said politely.

"Hi, this is Dan Prosky, calling for the senator."

"Dan!" Nancy almost shouted into the phone. "This is Nancy Drew!"

"Nancy—hey!" cried Dan. "What are you doing in town?"

"I'm working on a case, but I can't really talk about it. Sorry."

"That's okay, I understand. Listen, how's Bess?"

Bess and Dan had been very much interested in each other the last time Nancy and her friends were in D.C. It had looked like a budding romance—until the girls had headed back to River Heights. Dan hadn't called or written, much less come for a visit as he'd promised. Poor Bess had been inconsolable for about a week.

Then another cute guy had walked into her life, and she'd never mentioned Dan Prosky again. Still, Nancy knew Bess would have loved to see him.

"She's great, actually," Nancy replied.

"Not pining away for me?" Dan sounded disappointed.

"Well, she's no longer sitting at the window waiting for you to show up in River Heights," Nancy confessed. "And I can't say I blame her."

"It's my own fault that I haven't seen her, I guess," said Dan. He sounded remorseful. "I haven't been keeping in touch with anybody. It's a lot of work, being the senator's staffer, you know? And I thought I worked hard when I was a cop!"

"I know how hard you work, Dan," said Nancy. "Well, Marilyn's not here. Actually, she's been gone a long time, now that I think of it."

"Maybe she's trying to call you—I'll get off the line. Tell her I'll be over at nine tomorrow morning."

"Okay. Looking forward to seeing you. So long until then, Dan."

" 'Bye, Nancy."

Nancy hung up and looked at her watch. Marilyn had been gone for more than an hour. "I wonder what's taking Marilyn so long," she said to Teresa. "I hope she hasn't had any trouble finding the gun. I wonder if there was a snag—"

"Nancy," Teresa burst out, on the verge of

tears, "I don't want that gun in this apartment! I could not shoot anybody—not even my worst enemy."

Nancy put her arm around Teresa's shoulders and gave her a reassuring hug. "Don't worry, okay?" she said. "If you really don't want it here, Marilyn's not going to force it on you. She's just worried about you, that's all."

"I will talk to this woman, Beverly Bishop," Teresa said forcefully. "I will tell her she must keep silent!"

"It's no use," said Nancy. "You already tried."

"I do not understand."

"I went to see her today, pretending to be you, Teresa. She believed my act, but she told me to forget it. She's going to publish."

Just then the door burst open and Senator Kilpatrick came rushing in. "I tried to call you!" she said urgently. "The line was busy."

"Dan called, and we talked for a few minutes," Nancy explained. "But you've been gone for an hour and a half!"

"I had to take a walk to think."

Nancy looked closely at the senator. "What's wrong, Marilyn?"

The senator exhaled deeply. "Nancy, *the gun is gone!*"

Chapter

Six

MARILYN KILPATRICK PACED across the room, shaking her head. "I can't understand it. I mean, I couldn't have lost it. Not a *gun,* for goodness' sake!"

The senator stopped in the middle of the room and looked at the girls helplessly. "This is a nightmare. An utter nightmare," she groaned.

"Where could you have left it?" Nancy asked, taking charge.

"Nancy, I *know* I put it in my purse," Marilyn said, her voice firm. "I had it in my hand when you were in my office. Then I put it in the middle drawer of my desk, right? You saw me do that.

When I left for Beverly's, I slipped the gun into my purse, because I was going to bring it home tonight."

The senator sank down into a club chair, a dazed look on her face.

Teresa sat across from her older friend on the sofa, not saying a word, looking discouraged. Everything was going wrong for the two of them.

Walking to the mahogany bookcase that covered one wall, Nancy considered this new dark turn of events. Something in what Senator Kilpatrick was saying didn't make sense.

"Marilyn, a gun, even a small one, is pretty heavy," she said. "If it was missing from your purse, wouldn't you have felt the difference in weight?"

The senator sprang to her feet. "You're right!" she cried. "It *should* have been lighter—but it wasn't! I remember noticing how heavy my bag felt when I was at Beverly's."

"Where's the bag?" asked Nancy.

"Right here." Marilyn Kilpatrick carried the large navy purse over to Nancy. "Unless I'm losing my mind, it still feels heavy," she murmured.

Quickly, Nancy began searching the bag. Everything in it seemed harmless enough—a checkbook, a cosmetics bag, a package of tissues. But after a few seconds, Nancy pulled out a green glasses case.

"What's in this?" she asked, holding the case in her palm. It felt like a paperweight, it was so heavy.

"I carry sunglasses with me everywhere," the senator replied offhandedly.

Nancy weighed the case in her hand again. "I don't think so," she said. Then, snapping open the cover, she pulled out a gray rectangular bar. "Lead," announced Nancy grimly. "You didn't lose that revolver, Marilyn. Somebody took it out of your purse and planted this heavy bar so that you wouldn't notice the absence of the gun's weight."

Nancy thought of the threatening note Beverly Bishop had received, doused in the senator's perfume. Someone was trying to make Marilyn look like a criminal, or set her up for something. . . .

The senator sat down again, as if in slow motion, digesting the bitter truth. "But who?" she whispered. "Who would have done such a thing?"

"Did you stop anywhere on your way home?" Nancy inquired.

"Well, yes. I stopped for gas before I went to Beverly Bishop's office. You don't think Beverly could have stolen the revolver, do you? No, if she had seen the gun in my purse, she would have mentioned it in her book, not taken it."

"Anyplace else?" Nancy prompted her.

The older woman searched her mind, her large brown eyes narrowing. "After I left Beverly's, it was late, so I stopped to pick up our dinner. That's all."

"Now, let's see," Nancy mused. "Whoever took the gun must have known beforehand that you had it, otherwise they wouldn't have been prepared to plant the lead bar. That means it's not just simple theft. Marilyn, if I were you, I'd report that gun stolen right away."

"I suppose I have to," said the senator, picking up the phone, "although it's not going to look good in print, my owning a gun."

"A lot of public figures own guns. And it'll look much worse if you *don't* report it and it turns up."

"You're right, of course," agreed the senator, phoning the police. "Hello, this is Senator Marilyn Kilpatrick. I'd like to report a missing weapon."

She was doing the right thing, Nancy knew, but she couldn't help worrying. The gun might have been missing for several hours now—what if it had already been used?

"I'll make us some tea," Teresa said, standing up. "It will help us to—to calm down."

Nancy smiled at her friend and continued to sit on the sofa, trying to figure a way out of this mess. Now there were two problems to solve: the missing gun and the deadly chapters. The senator had probably never experienced a worse week in her life!

"There. That's that." When the phone was hung up a few minutes later, Nancy could tell the senator was feeling a little better. "All we can do now is hope it turns up."

"Marilyn," Teresa said softly, coming back from the kitchen with three cups of hot tea on a tray. "It's okay. I didn't want a gun in the apartment, anyway. Guns scare me. I've seen too many."

"I should have thought and never gotten it," the senator said, taking a cup and sipping the tea. "Thanks. This tastes good. By the way, what did Dan Prosky have to say?"

"He'll be here tomorrow morning at nine," Nancy replied. She put her cup down.

"Come on, now," Teresa said. "Let's talk about something else. We all need to get our minds off this, right?"

"Right!" echoed Senator Kilpatrick.

After the women had chatted for a while, Nancy said suddenly, "Oh, but wait a minute. Marilyn, Beverly Bishop is going to be on 'Late Night' at eleven-thirty. I read it in the TV section of the newspaper."

"She's probably going to plug her book," said the senator, leaning forward to flick on the TV.

The eleven o'clock news was on, and as the anchor introduced a story about a consumer recall of tainted milk in Virginia, Marilyn picked up the remote control and turned off the sound. "I think we have enough problems of our own," she said wryly, making Nancy and Teresa burst out giggling.

Suddenly a handsome man appeared on the screen. "It's Congressman Layton," announced Nancy, leaning forward in her seat. Matt Layton was certainly handsome, but Nancy noticed an arrogance in his mannerisms that made him less than attractive.

"Ugh," said Marilyn with a frown, reluctantly turning the sound back on. "I suppose I should hear what he's got to say," she said. "It's sure to be bad news—I spend half my time on Capitol Hill trying to undo the damage that guy does."

The voice of a network reporter filled the room: "Looking and sounding very much like a candidate for the Senate, Congressman Matt Layton today addressed a gathering of corporate leaders in downtown Washington, pushing his controversial economic reform program. As yet, he has not announced any plans to run against Senator Marilyn Kilpatrick in the next election, but political experts expect him to be a candidate. Tonight Layton stated that Senator Kilpatrick's approach is out-of-date and said that his own views are far more representative of the opinions of voters as a whole—"

"What nonsense," fumed the senator. "If it

weren't for his looks, he'd be a used-car salesman instead of a politician. He's the fastest talker I've ever heard—and believe me, there are a lot of them around here."

"And now for sports, here's Paul Sa—"

Marilyn pointed the remote at the TV, shutting the sound off again.

"Too bad you can't keep Layton quiet that easily, huh?" Nancy joked.

But the senator didn't find her joke funny. "The thing is, if Beverly Bishop ruins my reputation with that book of hers, Layton just *might* win my Senate seat," she admitted, sinking back into her chair, the furrow between her brows deeper than ever. "Not that I mind so much for myself, but it would be a real tragedy for the state I represent—and for the country as a whole."

Nancy couldn't help feeling the same way. Matt Layton could never replace Marilyn Kilpatrick; she was one of the most honest and compassionate people in office. Even now, with her career in jeopardy, she cared only about Teresa's safety and the welfare of the people she represented. She had always been like that, Nancy recalled. In all the years the Drews had known her, the senator had always thought of others before herself.

"Hey, there's a photograph of Beverly Bishop!" shouted Teresa. "Turn on the sound!"

"I've just been handed a news bulletin," said

the anchor solemnly. "Beverly Bishop, the well-known Washington columnist, was found dead tonight in her downtown office. Police are investigating, but the preliminary report says that Ms. Bishop appears to have been murdered. I repeat, Beverly Bishop is reported to have been murdered."

Chapter
Seven

B EVERLY BISHOP—MURDERED?" Teresa's voice shook.

"We'll be right back after these messages, with a recently taped interview with Beverly Bishop. See it all on 'Late Night' at eleven-thirty." The news commentator's voice was smooth and professional.

"I—I can't believe it," Marilyn Kilpatrick stammered, but she immediately recovered and went into action. "Nancy, get my car keys from the foyer, would you, please?" she asked, pressing the Record button on her VCR. "We can look at this interview later. Right now I think we should get over to Beverly's office. I want to be there if the police find my file so I can tell them about the danger Teresa will be in if its contents are made public. Teresa, you stay here. Don't forget to double-lock the door after we leave."

"I won't," Teresa mumbled, still a little stunned.

Nancy walked to the front door. She couldn't believe what had happened, either. Beverly Bishop, murdered! She had a feeling that the columnist's death was somehow related to the book she was about to publish.

"I'm ready, Marilyn!" Nancy called, holding up the senator's keys.

"Let's go, then. We should be back in a couple of hours, Teresa."

"'Bye," said Nancy, with a sympathetic look at the famous tennis player. "Don't open the door to anyone, okay?"

"I won't," Teresa said, and shuddered slightly.

The two women slipped outside and into the car. The senator maneuvered the vehicle out of her parking space, and Nancy reached over to turn on the radio. A report of Beverly Bishop's murder was sure to be on any news station.

An announcer's voice blared out of the car speakers with the gory details. "Bishop, known to her friends and enemies alike as 'the Poison Pen,'" he said, "was apparently alone, working late in her office at the time of the tragic incident. The police found her body slumped over the desk, with the mouthpiece of her Dictaphone in her hand. A security officer at the building reported that he heard a single gunshot at approximately ten P.M. Police theorize Ms. Bishop died instantly from the gunshot wound to her head.

"In other news, it was a big day for Baby R., the six-month-old Philadelphia infant who's at the center of a bitter dispute between—"

Nancy clicked off the news. She needed silence to think. Obviously a lot of people had wanted Beverly Bishop dead, and at least one had even threatened her in the past few hours. But who would actually have murdered her?

The streets of Washington were black and shiny from the light rain that had fallen earlier. As they sped along, Nancy glanced over at her friend. The senator looked extremely worried. Nancy realized she'd never seen Marilyn Kilpatrick that panicked before. Through all the troubles the high-powered politician had faced, she had always remained cool. Now her serenity was gone, and the senator was scared!

"Look at all these people," she said, stopping in front of Beverly Bishop's office building. A ring of police cars surrounded the entrance, and a crowd of reporters and photographers blocked their way. They pulled into the one available parking space and got out. Marilyn Kilpatrick flashed her Senate I.D. card to one of the young police officers on the sidewalk in front of the entrance.

"Go right up, Senator," he said, looking a little awestruck.

In seconds Nancy and Marilyn were walking up the stone steps to Beverly Bishop's newspaper office.

"Hold on, ladies," said a burly cop just inside the door. "No one except police allowed in."

"But the officer outside just told us we could go up," Nancy protested.

"I'm Senator Kilpatrick, and this is my assistant, Nancy Drew," Marilyn Kilpatrick said, trying to walk past before he could object again.

The officer held out his arm to stop her. "This is a police matter, Senator—not an affair of state. I can't let you in. Sorry."

"Officer, I assure you, it's a very urgent matter—" Across the lobby, the elevator doors opened, and a grizzled man in a rumpled gray suit stepped out. The senator cut her words short.

"Someone I know—the head of the homicide squad," she whispered to Nancy. "Captain Flynn!" she called.

The man stared in surprise. "Senator Kilpatrick! What are you doing here?"

"I'm certainly glad we ran into you," she said, stepping past the door guard to take Captain Flynn's arm. She led him aside, talking urgently in a low voice.

The captain shook his head as he listened, his

face unhappy. Finally he said, "All right, Senator. You can come up for a look—on two conditions. First, nothing leaves the scene of the crime."

Flynn gave the woman a stern look. "And second, do me a favor—keep a low profile. It's a zoo up there, with all my people and the medical examiner's. Let's see if that elevator is still here. Mike," he said to the policeman at the entrance, "if anyone asks, they're with me." His voice reverberated through the marble lobby.

"Captain Flynn, I'd like you to meet Nancy Drew. Nancy's visiting me for a while, helping me out with a few things," the senator explained when the three of them were inside the elevator.

"Nancy Drew! That's a name I'll never forget, not after the way you helped that tennis player a while back. What was her name—Montenegro?"

"That's right," Nancy answered.

"Well, pleased to meet you, Ms. Drew. You really do look just like her, don't you?" The captain shook his head in wonder.

"That's what they tell me," Nancy said with a smile.

Just then the elevator doors opened and Nancy, Marilyn Kilpatrick, and Captain Flynn stepped into a dimly lit hallway.

Two police officers were stationed outside the columnist's office, but when Captain Flynn appeared, they stepped aside to let him in. "These women are with me," he announced. Marilyn and Nancy, with a nod to the officers, followed close behind.

Inside the writer's office, a police team was busy dusting the place for prints and marking areas with thick white tape. Beverly's body lay on the floor where she had fallen. It was covered with a white sheet with only the feet showing.

While the others worked, Nancy stood off to the side, scrutinizing the grisly scene. One of the corpse's stiletto-heeled shoes was askew. The heel was dangling, as if it had twisted and nearly broken off, perhaps when the columnist fell from her chair. How odd, Nancy thought. That morning she had noticed what an impeccable dresser Beverly was, the type who wore things once and then put them away. Her shoes had looked brand-new, and they were obviously very expensive. So why would the heel come off so easily?

"We checked, and there was no sign of forced entry," Captain Flynn was explaining to an eager young district attorney. "That indicates that she was probably killed by an acquaintance, someone who knew she was here all alone. Also, as far as we can tell, robbery was not a motive. Whoever killed her left all her cash and jewelry intact. There's only one thing missing."

The police captain walked over to the columnist's desk and flipped open the Dictaphone with a dramatic flair. "You see, she must have been dictating when the perpetrator arrived—the microphone was in her hand, and the machine was still warm when we arrived. But look at this."

The captain pointed inside the machine. "Empty," he declared.

"Captain Flynn, what about her files?" the district attorney asked. "They must have been loaded with explosive information, the kind people murder for."

"That was the first thing we checked. You want to see something incredible?" asked Flynn, walking to the metal file cabinets behind the desk. "Take a look at this!"

He opened a drawer and pulled out a bright red snakeskin belt. "Beverly Bishop was quite a character," he observed. "These file cabinets are full of accessories. She's got scarves, belts, hats, you name it. The only pencil in here is an eyebrow pencil. There's not a scrap of paper, no computer disks, no information of any kind.

"According to her secretary and everyone else who knew about this office, she didn't keep files. All her work was on tape or in her head, and we haven't found any tapes. We checked here, and we've got people searching her home as well. But so far, nothing." With that, and a shake of his head, he deftly pushed the metal drawers shut.

Again Nancy thought back to her interview with Beverly Bishop. What was it the columnist had said? She had finished three of the last four chapters. Two were already typed out, and she'd planned to complete the third that afternoon and send all but the final one to the publisher that day! That meant three chapters were en route by now. So there was only one chance in four that the killer had found what he or she wanted on the Dictaphone tape.

"Anything else you want to know?" Flynn looked around the room at everybody.

Just the identity of that fourth person, Nancy said to herself. That's all.

"Motive seems clear in the case of someone called the Poison Pen," the D.A. reflected.

"I know what I forgot to tell you," Flynn announced, smacking his forehead with the heel of his hand. "The perfume. The security guard said the place stank of perfume when he got here. I sent him down to the lab to test some fragrances to see if he could identify the brand."

The senator cast Nancy a nervous glance. If the perfume had been Worth, it would implicate her in the murder—especially when the police discovered the perfumed threat note. They both knew it. And the politician's missing gun would only make her more of a suspect. Nancy wondered if she should call her father. If the police didn't find the real culprit, Marilyn was going to need a good lawyer—soon.

"So we know it's a woman," said Flynn confidently.

"I think you may be jumping to conclusions, Captain. A man might have worn a woman's perfume to throw us off his trail," the D.A. objected.

"Maybe." The captain shrugged. "But we also have this." Pulling a clean handkerchief out of his pocket, he walked over to the other side of the room and opened a police-department exhibit case. "We found this little sweetheart, and it's definitely what you'd call a woman's weapon."

With that, he reached into the case and pulled out a small revolver. A revolver that looked just like the one that Marilyn Kilpatrick had lost.

Chapter
Eight

NANCY QUICKLY GLANCED over at Marilyn out of the corner of her eye. The senator showed only the faintest glimmer of surprise, but Nancy knew that she had to be dying inside. Whoever was out to frame Marilyn Kilpatrick was doing an excellent job of it.

When the police traced the gun and found that it was registered to the senator, her political career would be finished forever. Even worse, she might have to go to jail! Nancy couldn't even say for sure that the politician was innocent; she had disappeared for a long time that evening, and she had no way of proving where she'd been.

"Well, Captain, I guess we'll get out of your

way," Marilyn Kilpatrick said in a faint voice. "Thank you for letting me take a look around."

"Okay, Senator. Take care. Nice to meet you, Ms. Drew." The police captain threw the two women a friendly smile and waved quickly before he turned back to his work.

The senator, with Nancy right behind her, bolted out of the room and walked briskly to the elevator, her eyes straight ahead. Once they made it downstairs and outside, she let out a huge sigh of relief. "I'm glad we got out of there," she told Nancy as they walked down the stone steps toward the crowd of reporters and police officers. "It made me so nervous, being in there with that—that woman's corpse!"

Just then a woman who had been hurrying up the stairs of the building toward them stopped. Nancy recognized her immediately. It was Jillian Riley, hot on the trail of her latest scoop.

"Senator, I thought you never got nervous," she commented wickedly. "Is something wrong?" Chuckling, she continued up the steps and flung open the door.

The two friends hurried down the stairs to their car. "It's okay, Marilyn," Nancy assured the older woman. "She doesn't know anything, believe me." Nancy didn't believe it herself, but she had to calm the senator down somehow.

"This is a nightmare!" The senator's voice broke the silence as she raced her car toward her apartment. "An absolute nightmare! Nancy, who's going to believe that I had nothing to do with all this? Can you imagine what the press will do to me? And what if Matt Layton finds out about this? He'll eat me alive! What if that gun *was* mine—you know it has to be!"

In spite of herself, Nancy winced. Things were really looking bad. It was as if all the senator's problems were multiplying before their eyes.

Teresa Montenegro's life was still in danger, and now the career and reputation Marilyn Kilpatrick had earned for herself were about to be destroyed, too. And one person was dead. Nancy leaned back into the leather-upholstered passenger seat and tried to think. There had to be a clue, a piece of information that would show how everything fit together and who was behind all this ugly activity, and why. Who hated Beverly Bishop enough to murder her? Or who hated Marilyn Kilpatrick enough to frame her for murder?

"The worst part is, I don't even have an alibi!" the senator moaned. "There I was, alone in my office, while Beverly Bishop was being murdered with my gun. No one will believe *that* in court."

The senator pulled into a parking space in front of her apartment building and got out of the car. The two women walked inside in silence. Marilyn slipped her key into the door of her apartment and sighed. "I wish this day would just end," she admitted.

When the door opened, Teresa jumped up

from the sofa. "Thank goodness you're back. What happened? Did you find the files? Is everything okay?" The expression on her pretty face flitted between fear and hope.

The senator fidgeted with her keys when she answered. "I'm afraid not, Teresa. There wasn't anything to get. Beverly Bishop didn't keep any files. She kept the book in her head, or she sent it on to her publisher."

Teresa dropped her gaze to the floor. "So there is nothing to be done."

"Well, that's not all," the politician went on bleakly. "Please fill her in, Nancy. I'm too upset."

Reluctantly, Nancy looked straight at Teresa and told her the awful news. "Beverly Bishop was killed with the same type of revolver Marilyn bought for you. Since the senator's gun is missing, it's very likely that someone is trying to frame her," she explained.

"No!" Teresa gasped. "But why?"

"That's what we've got to find out," said Nancy.

As Senator Kilpatrick lowered herself onto the rose-colored sofa in the living room, she looked utterly defeated. "You know," she said sadly, "I've always prided myself on not having enemies. I like to keep my relationships, both personal and professional, harmonious, even with political opponents. I know not everyone agreed with all of my views, but I never dreamed anybody felt such hostility toward me. I guess I was wrong. . . ." The senator nervously smoothed a hand over her auburn hair.

"Marilyn," Nancy interjected, sitting down next to her. "We're not giving up. I'm going to get to the bottom of this, I promise—but I'll need assistance."

"I can help you, Nancy!" cried Teresa. "You've helped me so much that I'd be happy to—"

"No, Teresa." Nancy shook her head. "You've got to stay in hiding. Your life might be in danger. Until we find out what's going on, I want you to keep a low profile. Besides, I need someone who's experienced. Marilyn, is there any chance of involving Dan Prosky with the case? I know he's supposed to be guarding Teresa, but I've got an awful lot of ground to cover, and not much time. Can't we find somebody else to stay with Teresa? I know I can rely on Dan."

The senator took a long look at Nancy. Then she massaged her temples as if she had a bad headache. "Nancy—Dan Prosky thinks the world of me. He doesn't know I bribed people in San Carlos to get Teresa out, and I just can't imagine what he'd say if he learned the truth. He used to be with the police, and— Oh, I don't know. Maybe I should just hold a press conference and tell the whole world what's going on. My career could be ruined, but at least I wouldn't have to hide it anymore. If it wouldn't endanger Teresa's life, I'd do it this minute!"

But calling in the press at a time like this was out of the question, and they all knew it.

"How's this for an idea?" Nancy said, brightening for a minute. "We'll keep Dan in the dark, for as long as possible, anyway. Maybe we can find the killer before we have to explain the whole San Carlos affair."

After a tiny hesitation, the senator responded. "I guess I can live with that," she muttered. "I'll call Dan and ask him to come over right away. And I'll get another bodyguard to take care of Teresa."

"I am so sorry I bring you such trouble, Marilyn—after all you have done—" Teresa's eyes were filled with unshed tears.

"Never mind that," the senator replied. "I don't know how she's going to do it, but I have faith in this girl to get us out of this." She put an arm on Nancy's shoulder. "She can work miracles, as we all know."

Nancy blushed and shook her head. "As long as we stick together, we'll do fine. You've got to remember that. It takes teamwork," she said.

"Okay. I'm sold," said the senator, standing up. "I'd better make the calls to get you some help," she said as she left the room.

Nancy went over to the VCR and rewound the videotape, which had been recording ever since they had left.

"I didn't want to touch any of the buttons," Teresa confided. "I was afraid I would break it."

"This is really going to be bizarre," said Nancy, as she pushed the Play button and sat down to watch the murdered woman's last TV interview. A little shiver slid down her spine as the image of Beverly Bishop walked across the set to be interviewed by the talk show host. They had filmed the show late that afternoon, and now the columnist was just another body on the way to the morgue. Nancy and Teresa sat on the floor in front of the TV, eyes riveted to the screen.

The senator stepped back into the living room and sank into a chair close to the TV set. "Dan's on his way over now. He wants us to fill him in," she whispered.

"Good evening, ladies and gentlemen, and welcome to 'Late Night.' You all know Beverly Bishop—one of this town's most famous and most controversial columnists. Beverly, do you consider yourself a *gossip* columnist? Or is *gossip* a bad word these days?" Jim Long, the young blond talk show host, leaned toward the woman he was to interview.

Beverly Bishop smiled mischievously. "It's always been a bad word, Jim," she replied, "but I don't mind being called a gossip columnist. I've never cared much what other people thought of me—except my readers, of course."

"She doesn't seem like a nice person, does she?" mumbled Teresa.

"Beverly," said Long, "everyone wants to know about your new book." He looked directly into the camera. "For those of you out there who were born yesterday, the book is called *Tell Me Everything*. Several people have predicted that it will be a blockbuster, and I hear that the rumors about the book's contents have sent several well-known Washingtonians into hiding."

Beverly smiled again. "You said it, Jim, I didn't. But if my book isn't number one on the best-seller list, I'll drop dead of shock!"

Laughter followed from the audience. Nancy couldn't help noticing how ironic it was that the columnist's last interview had been about this "blockbuster" book. The book had killed her, in effect. Nancy stared at the columnist, fascinated.

"So come on, we're all friends here, Beverly. Tell *us* everything," Jim Long quipped. "Who's going to be run out of town when this volume of information hits the stands?"

Beverly's devilish smile grew even wider. She crossed her legs and put her hands pertly on her knee. "Well, I'm not going to say *too* much, Jim," she taunted him, "but I will tell you this. The 'big four' had better start packing, and you know who you are!" She gave a throaty laugh. "Seriously, though, I've just finished three of the last four chapters, and they're on the way to my publisher, Pringle Press, right now. I'll finish the fourth tonight, and the book should be out in less than a month."

"What do you want to bet I'm one of the so-called big four?" moaned the senator.

"I'm sure you are," agreed Nancy. "But what we care about is who the other three are. One of them framed you, and we've got to nab him or her before the police arrest you!"

"You see, Jim, certain people in Washington pride themselves on their so-called integrity. But when you scratch the surface, you find out that these people are as sleazy as everybody else. And I think the little people have a right to know it," the columnist went on.

"This is making me sick," said Marilyn. "Beverly's talking about me, which won't make me seem any less suspicious. Everyone knows I stand for honesty and integrity. With her hurling insults at me, and my gun as the possible murder weapon . . ." She broke off, not wanting to finish the awful thought. "Oh, well. At least I reported the gun being stolen."

Nancy didn't say what she was thinking—that Marilyn had called to report the missing gun *after* the murder had occurred. No need to worry her friend further, Nancy thought.

"Well, there can't be too much more," the senator said. She picked up the remote from the floor. "Maybe we should see if there's an old movie on. Anything but watch this wicked—"

"Hold it!" Nancy suddenly cried out, spotting something. "Marilyn, wind the tape back just a little—no, too far—stop! Yes, right there. Now play it in slow motion."

Nancy studied the moment that had caught her

eye. Her legs crossed, the columnist was talking up a storm. As Nancy watched, she saw her absentmindedly reach down to touch the stiletto heel of her left shoe. While she spoke, Beverly fiddled with the heel for at least fifteen seconds.

"That's it!" Nancy blurted out. "I knew there was something weird about that!"

"About what?" asked the other two. But before Nancy could reply, the doorbell rang.

"That'll be Dan," Teresa said, going to answer it.

Nancy jumped up from the floor. She grabbed her purse off the sofa and headed straight for the front door.

"Hi, what's up?" asked Dan Prosky, stepping over the threshold into the foyer. "Nancy," he said, smiling broadly. "Good to see you again."

"Never mind!" Nancy said, grabbing his arm and yanking him back out the door as a stunned Marilyn and Teresa watched.

"Come on, Dan—we're going on a little trip," Nancy told him.

"Huh? Where to, Nancy?" asked Dan, startled. "It's two-thirty in the morning."

"To the morgue, Dan—and pronto!"

Chapter
Nine

"THE MORGUE!" DAN looked back over his shoulder at the senator for confirmation.

"Do as she says, Dan. Nancy will explain in the car."

"All right—whatever you say, Senator." Dan followed Nancy to the curb and opened the door of his blue government-issue sedan for Nancy.

Once they had fastened their seat belts, Dan pulled the car out onto the street to head downtown. Nancy turned to Dan. "Have you heard about Beverly Bishop?" she asked.

Dan nodded and let out a low whistle. News spread fast in Washington, even in the middle of the night.

"Well, someone is trying to pin the murder on Senator Kilpatrick," explained Nancy. She quickly filled Dan in on the details of the frame. "And that's why I've got to have a look at Beverly's body," she concluded. "Got it so far?"

"I think so." Dan's wide gray eyes were troubled. "That's some pretty heavy stuff."

He was silent for a moment, his face clouding over as he turned off the Beltway and headed toward the morgue. "Nancy, I've got to know something—and please give me a straight answer. How did the senator get mixed up in all this? Did she do something wrong?" he asked softly.

"No, she didn't, Dan," answered Nancy firmly, speaking from her heart. "But maybe she did something *extralegal,* if you know what I mean. Something that saved an innocent life, but wouldn't look too good in print."

"Oh, come on. You're not afraid to tell me just because I'm an ex-cop, are you?" he asked, smiling.

"Dan, if you want to know anything more, you'll have to ask the senator. I'm sure she'll fill you in," said Nancy with a tone of finality. "Could you drive a little faster? I'm afraid somebody's going to get there before we do."

"Hey, Nancy," said Dan with a big grin. "In case you haven't noticed, we *are* the only people crazy enough to be headed for the morgue right now."

"Maybe. But you never know," said Nancy. "Not when the body belongs to a columnist like Beverly Bishop."

The morgue attendant seemed grateful for the company when Dan and Nancy arrived. "Dan Prosky! How are you? I haven't seen you in a long time."

"That's because I quit the force," answered Dan. "But I wondered if you could let me see something, anyway. It's kind of important."

"Sure, sure. Come in." The attendant walked them to an area with comfortable chairs.

"Nancy Drew, this is Walt Kinsky. Walt and I went to college together," Dan explained.

"Yeah, but I graduated," Walt said teasingly.

"Hi, Walt." Nancy smiled.

"Nice to meet you. So, how can I help you, old buddy? Who did you come to visit this time?"

"Beverly Bishop," Dan said seriously.

Walt let out a low whistle. "Isn't that something? The doctor just left her body here. I guess she knew one secret too many. Well, come in. Nancy, would you like to wait out here?"

"Thank you, but I'd rather take a look at her, I think." Nancy tried to restrain her impatience. Walt didn't know how urgent this was.

"Nancy's not exactly fainthearted," Dan replied as they followed Walt down a dimly lit hallway.

"Well, suit yourselves." Walt pushed open a thick hydraulic door and led Dan and Nancy into the vaults.

Banks of rectangular doors stood against three of the walls, and the room was extremely cold. Nancy couldn't help shuddering for a second. Morgues weren't her favorite places, but if she could get information that would help save her friends, she could put up with the chemical smell and the frigid atmosphere for a few minutes.

"Here we go," Walt announced. "Number four thirty-four—Bishop."

Inserting a key into a small brass lock, he pulled out the rolling bier. There was the form of Beverly Bishop, covered by a sheet stamped with the city's seal.

"Actually, it's her clothing that we'd really like to look at," Nancy suggested.

"That's in the drawer right under here," said Walt, shoving the bier closed and locking it. "We have to impound all the accessories," he explained, opening the second drawer. "It's mostly just clothes."

Nancy looked down and saw a flash of electric blue. It was the dress Beverly Bishop had been wearing that night on TV. Next to the folded dress was a pair of black patent leather high-heeled shoes. They were the same shoes Nancy had seen Beverly wearing on "Late Night."

"Here we are. Dress, stockings, shoes—et

cetera. Look, would you guys like some coffee? I put some on just before you got here," Walt offered.

"Great, I'd love some. You, Nancy?" asked Dan, walking away with his friend. He seemed to sense Nancy's need to be alone for a minute, and she was grateful.

"No, thanks," said Nancy. As soon as the two men left the room, she began concentrating on Beverly Bishop's things. Carefully pulling the sleeves of her sweater down around her hands to avoid leaving fingerprints, Nancy picked up Beverly Bishop's left shoe and examined it. She gripped the heel and twisted it slightly, as the columnist had done during her interview with Jim Long. To Nancy's surprise, it turned in her hand, almost like a door handle. The heel swung open, revealing a tiny compartment just under the sole of the shoe. Her pulse quickening, she held the shoe in one hand and poked the index finger of her other hand up into the tiny box. She felt something small and metal, which fell out into her palm when she shook the shoe.

Nancy looked down, her blue eyes widening. It was a key!

As Dan pulled his car out of the parking lot and onto the deserted avenue, Nancy clutched the tiny key in one hand. It was small and blunt, obviously the key to a locker or a piece of luggage. Now she had to find what it fit. That wouldn't be easy, but it was a start.

What key would be so crucial to Beverly Bishop that she carried it around with her, hidden in her shoe? It was probably related to work, Nancy thought, since that seemed to be her life. The police captain had said that he'd searched her office for files, but that she apparently hadn't kept any.

Maybe that was what she *wanted* everyone to think—it fit in with the image of the know-it-all columnist. Beverly Bishop *couldn't* keep all that information in her head, but it was so secret that she stored it far from her office so that no one would ever come across it.

Well, she had succeeded. Now she was dead, and the only person who knew about the key was Nancy. There had to be hundreds of lockers in Washington, D.C. Somewhere, maybe, one of them contained the files on the big four.

Nancy would find that missing file if she put her mind to it. Then she'd know for sure who else—besides Marilyn Kilpatrick—Beverly Bishop had been ready to expose.

That thought made her feel better. She leaned back in her seat and smiled, watching the lights of Washington go by. "This sure is a lot different from the last time we took a drive together," she commented, thinking back to the time when the death squads from San Carlos had pursued them through the streets.

Dan let out a laugh. "Yeah, that was a little too exciting, even for me. Car chases are strictly for TV. My life is interesting enough without defying death, know what I mean?"

"I sure do." As she stared out the window, Nancy glanced at the passenger sideview mirror.

There was a car right behind them, but of course, that in itself meant nothing. And even though the Washington grapevine seemed to buzz with lightning speed, there was no way that someone would have already heard about their trip to the morgue.

Still, at four in the morning, with so few cars on the deserted Washington streets, it did seem strange that someone would tailgate them.

Nancy looked out at the mirror a few seconds later. The same car was there. Just to make sure, she said, "Dan, could you turn off here?"

"Sure." As he turned the corner and accelerated, the lights of the other car followed.

"I can't believe this," Nancy murmured, her eyes glued to the sideview mirror.

"What's the matter?" asked Dan. "Uh-oh. Someone's behind us."

"Yes, it looks as if we're being followed." Nancy sighed. "This has been the longest day of my life."

Dan glanced up at the rearview mirror as he took another right turn, then shook his head. "That car *is* tagging us," he said. "Hold on to your seat, Nancy." He floored the accelerator.

Dan's car peeled out, leaving their pursuers behind. But in the next instant, with a screech of burning rubber, the second car took off in hot pursuit.

Nancy stuck her head out the window, trying to get a glimpse, an outline of a face, a head, a license plate—anything. With the car's bright headlights in her face, it was impossible. Then a metallic flash coming out of the side window caught her eye. A gun! She ducked her head back into the car just as a bullet whizzed by. A second bullet shattered the passenger sideview mirror.

Both Dan and Nancy slid down as low as they could in their seats to stay out of range of the next shots. Dan took a sharp right, then a sharp left, then another right down an alley and a left onto the next street. Behind them they heard the other car's tires screeching as it negotiated the quick turns. Instead of dropping back, the car drew closer.

As they raced up the hill into Georgetown, Nancy began to worry. The streets were so deserted that there was no way to lose their pursuer —nor would there be any witnesses if something happened. She and Dan had to win this battle on their own.

Pulling around a sharp corner, Dan gritted his teeth and braked to a sudden stop.

"Now!" he cried. "Get out, quick!"

Nancy flung open the door, jumped out onto the street, and quickly dashed between two parked cars. Immediately Dan pressed the accelerator and the car took off down the street, the passenger door slamming shut on its own.

Nancy's heart pounded wildly, and she gasped for breath. Would their enemies, whoever they were, fall for Dan's ploy? There was nothing she could do but try to stay hidden between the parked cars. And hope she'd be safe.

About two seconds later the other car stopped right in front of her hiding place. "I'm telling you, she got out here!" said a gruff voice, as the door of the car opened and a large, dark form emerged. Whoever he was, he looked too big for Nancy to fight on her own. She heard the door slam shut again, and the car sped off after Dan.

There was silence for a few seconds, and then Nancy heard footsteps on the cobblestone street. If only she could have peeked out for one second, long enough to catch the license number! But she couldn't risk being found.

Nancy heard footsteps move in different directions as the man searched for her. Please don't find me, she prayed. But the footsteps were circling in on her, closer and closer. Crouching even farther down, she could see the man's shoes on the other side of the car—shiny two-toned brown loafers with tassels. Any second now, he'd discover her hiding place!

Just then there came the hair-raising sound of screeching brakes from a few blocks away. The footsteps stopped, and so did Nancy's breathing as both she and her pursuer listened to the sickening crash and the explosion that followed.

Nancy's heart leapt into her throat as she saw a huge fireball rising in the sky.

There were only two cars going that fast at four in the morning, and Dan had been driving one of them. Had he gotten out in time? Flames surged skyward in the darkness. There was no way anyone could have survived that accident.

Dan had to be dead.

Chapter

Ten

NANCY WATCHED HER pursuer's legs from between the wheels of the parked car. He hesitated a moment before sprinting off in the direction of the explosion.

When Nancy thought it was safe, she stood up.

Smoke rose in a huge pillar straight up in the windless dawn sky. Windows were being thrown open up and down the block, and people were shouting to one another, asking what had happened.

Nancy wanted desperately to run down the street, to see what had happened, to find Dan—if Dan was still there to find.

One person had already died—maybe two. That was enough. If she went there now, the thug would probably still be hanging around, looking for her. Besides, there was nothing she could do for Dan now. She heard sirens getting closer, so someone had already called the fire department, the police, and the hospital.

Nancy thought about Dan. He had dropped her off not even ten minutes ago, and now . . . He had only been trying to help her. If she hadn't insisted that they go to the morgue in the middle of the night, he'd still be— *Stop it!* Nancy ordered herself. She couldn't afford to mourn, not now. She had to get on with the case. She started walking casually away from the area, breathing deeply and massaging her tired eyes and temples. She went down street after street, searching for a familiar landmark as the sun rose. Her bag with the all-important key in it was slung over her shoulder.

After a while she came to a small coffee shop just opening for breakfast. Nancy went in and ordered a cup of coffee. She wasn't much of a coffee drinker, but she'd been up all night, and she needed to stay awake awhile longer yet. It was all she could do to keep from putting her head on the table and collapsing into a deep sleep, but she had to put the pieces of the puzzle together, she just had to.

The waitress set the coffee cup on the counter

in front of Nancy. Just staring at the steaming liquid and smelling the aroma seemed to wake her up. She took a sip and began to go over everything in her mind.

The big four. Marilyn Kilpatrick, Della Hawks, Jillian Riley, and—who? Which one had murdered Beverly Bishop?

She remembered the wildly beautiful face and the hot temper of Della Hawks, young wife of old Justice Hawks. She had threatened the columnist's life, right in front of Nancy. What could Beverly Bishop have had on her? There could be any number of skeletons in her closet. Nancy made a mental note to find out all she could about Mrs. Hawks. She could skim old gossip columns on microfilm at the library, or possibly arrange a meeting with Della Hawks herself.

What about Marilyn Kilpatrick? She'd known Nancy was going to the morgue in the middle of the night, and she had taken desperate measures to get Teresa into the United States. Was she desperate about other things, too?

Nancy dismissed the wild thought that had crept into her head. The senator had *invited* her to come to Washington. Why, Nancy's father had known her for years!

Someone was clearly trying to frame her, but why?

Nancy fished in her bag for the key, brought it out, and looked at it closely. The number on it was 663. Somewhere in Washington, Beverly Bishop had kept a locker full of secrets—but where? A health club? The bus station?

Nancy put the key back into her purse; that search would have to wait. First she had to go to Beverly Bishop's publisher and try to intercept the three chapters that were on the way. She didn't know how she'd do it, but she had to at least try—for Teresa and Marilyn.

Tossing a dollar bill onto the counter, Nancy stood up and walked out of the coffee shop. As she hit the sidewalk, she noticed the faint smell of smoke in the early morning air. Oh, Dan, she thought. I hope there's been a miracle. I hope you're still alive!

Nancy caught a taxi back to the apartment. Not wanting to disturb the others at that hour of the morning, she took a quick, quiet sponge bath and changed into fresh clothes. Since she was planning to impersonate Teresa for the second day in a row, she needed to look as neat and together as the tennis star always did.

Before leaving the apartment, Nancy scrawled a quick note, saying that she was okay and explaining that she'd be back later that morning. At this point, Nancy didn't want to tell the senator any more than she had to.

On the way over to Pringle Press, Nancy stopped at another coffee shop for breakfast, and lots of coffee this time.

Desperate to find out if Dan was okay, Nancy went to the coffee shop's pay phone and called several of the city's hospitals, but none of them had admitted a patient by that name. It either meant Dan had escaped injury—or he was dead.

Half an hour later Nancy was riding the gleaming chrome elevator to the fourteenth floor of the Pringle Press Building. Then, quickly and silently reviewing her Teresa Montenegro imitation, she opened the glass door of Pringle Press and strode confidently up to the receptionist.

"Pardon me." She adopted a hint of a Spanish accent and addressed the middle-aged woman with horn-rimmed glasses who sat behind the desk. "I would like to speak with the president of the company as soon as she arrives, please."

The woman looked her up and down. "Ms. Pringle will be in shortly. Do you have an appointment?"

"Uh, no, I do not have one, but this is an emergency. I think she will see me."

"Mm-hm." The woman did not look at all convinced. "May I have your name, please?" She picked up a ballpoint pen to write it down.

"My name is Teresa Montenegro. *M-O-N-T—*"

The woman dropped her pen and quickly adjusted her glasses. "You're the famous tennis player!" She coughed in embarrassment. "I'm sorry, Ms. Montenegro. I should have recognized you. Why, I've seen you play dozens of times! I'm certain Ms. Pringle will be delighted to see you. She's a great fan of yours, too."

The receptionist was about to go on, but just then a man opened the door and walked in. "Oh, excuse me—here's the morning mail. Hi, Johnny. Johnny, you're not going to believe it, but this is Teresa Montenegro, the tennis player!"

The mailman looked up at Nancy. "Nice to meet you, miss," he said. "Actually, I'm more of a hockey fan myself," he added, apologizing for not knowing who she was. He dumped a huge bundle of envelopes and magazines onto the receptionist's desk. "Have a nice day, everyone," he said, heading out the door.

Nancy stared at the stack. Were Beverly Bishop's chapters in there? There was no way to find out with the receptionist in the room. Could she distract the woman somehow? No, too risky.

With a sigh, Nancy decided to stick to her original plan: a personal appeal to the publisher herself. If Ms. Pringle really was a big fan of Teresa's, that could be a help.

"Well, Ms. Montenegro," said the receptionist. "I'll just go put these on Ms. Pringle's desk. Make yourself at home, and I'll be back in just a moment."

Nancy tried hard to stay calm, but just knowing the means to save her friends might be in that stack of mail was driving her crazy.

Something caught Nancy's eye, and she realized a boy was standing in the doorway. She'd been so lost in thought that she hadn't even heard the door open.

"Messenger service," said the boy. He had a huge green bag slung over one shoulder. "Sign right here," he said, holding out the package and a clipboard with a form on it.

Nancy was about to say that she didn't work there when she spotted the return address on the package. It was from Beverly Bishop!

"Um, where do I sign?" asked Nancy, glancing over her shoulder to see if the receptionist was coming.

"Right there." The boy pointed to a line, and Nancy quickly and illegibly initialed his form.

"You new here?" asked the boy.

"Yes, it's my first day," Nancy answered, without skipping a beat. And my last, she added silently. "Well—thank you. Have a nice day."

"Yeah, you, too. See you around."

Nancy breathed a sigh of relief when the boy disappeared into the elevator. Then she stuffed the thick envelope into her bag, which was big enough to hold the bulky package without bulging suspiciously.

Nancy dropped back into her seat just as the receptionist breezed back into the room. Swiftly she crossed her legs, trying to look as casual as possible.

"Were you talking to someone?" asked the receptionist. "I thought I heard someone come in."

Nancy thought fast. "Just somebody looking for the ladies' room," she explained. "Speaking of which, is there one around here? I would like to freshen up before I see Ms. Pringle."

"Certainly. It's right down the hall on your left. You'll need this key." She handed Nancy a key on an enormous ring.

Nancy had to restrain herself from rushing down the hall. Soon she would know the identities of three of the big four—and maybe she'd learn why one of them had had to kill Beverly Bishop!

Quickly unlocking the door, Nancy stepped inside the bathroom. Luckily, she was the only one there. Nancy locked herself into a stall and pulled the manila envelope out of her bag. She slowly drew out the chapters. There were three, each secured with a giant paper clip.

Nancy's eye roved over the front page of the first. "Senator Marilyn Kilpatrick" was typed across the top in boldface. No surprises there, but Nancy was glad to have the chapter in her hand and away from the printing presses.

Nancy flipped to the second chapter: "Mrs. Della Hawks." She would definitely have to check into the mysterious Mrs. Hawks's past.

Moving on to the last chapter, Nancy held her

breath. She turned the page, and there was the third name—"Jillian Riley." Just as Jillian herself had expected, Beverly had desperately wanted to ruin her rival's career.

But, mused Nancy, perhaps Jillian had decided to end Beverly Bishop's career first—by killing her!

Chapter

Eleven

MURDER: THE PERFECT ending to a vicious, career-long rivalry. Nancy remembered seeing Jillian at the scene of the crime, hurrying to get the scoop on her competitor's death. Jillian could have killed Beverly Bishop and framed the senator for it. Now she could write a best-selling story about Marilyn Kilpatrick's brutal murder of the woman who knew too much—Nancy could almost see the headlines. Jillian had the power to convince everyone in the city that Marilyn was guilty, if she wanted to.

Nancy wondered what she should do with the envelope. If she returned the chapters, they would almost certainly be published. On the other hand, if she turned them over to the police, the senator might be in even bigger trouble. Before Nancy made up her mind, the door to the ladies' room opened and someone came in.

Suddenly her safe nest had been invaded, and Nancy had to get out. As soon as the feet entered a stall and closed the door, Nancy stuffed the chapters back into her bag and emerged from her hiding place.

Deciding it would be best to return the chapters while she worked on solving the mystery of the fourth suspect, Nancy walked up to the main door of Pringle Press. She hoped that the receptionist wouldn't notice her slip the envelope under the door. To her surprise, there was someone else in the room—a man, with his back to her, talking to the receptionist. As Nancy brushed back a wisp of hair from her face, she saw the man's shoes—

Shiny two-toned brown tasseled loafers! Nancy's mind shot back a few hours to that street in Georgetown—those shoes were the same ones she had glimpsed between the parked cars!

Not wanting to take any chances, Nancy hung the ladies' room key on the doorknob, turned around, headed for the elevators, and stuffed the envelope back into her bag.

Leaving the building, Nancy cast glances in every direction to make sure she wasn't being followed. She'd have to call to cancel Teresa's meeting with the publisher. But she'd been lucky to spot that character before he'd seen her. Of course she didn't know if he would recognize her on sight, or if he even knew who she was.

"Taxi!" she called, waving her arm as a cab drove past the building. It stopped a few yards away, and Nancy ran up and clambered in.

If someone was following her, it would have been impossible to tell. The morning rush-hour crowds were thinning along Pennsylvania Avenue, but there were still dozens of people on the street. Nancy constantly checked out the back window of the cab all the way to the apartment. Nothing. At least she couldn't *see* anything.

When she walked in the front door, Nancy heard the senator talking in the kitchen. Maybe she and Teresa were lingering over breakfast.

Instead, she found Captain Flynn sitting at the kitchen table with the senator, drinking a cup of coffee and eating a doughnut. He gave Nancy a friendly but sober greeting.

"Morning, Ms. Drew," he said.

"Morning, Captain," Nancy replied. "What's up?"

The policeman's face looked grim. "I was just telling the senator here that we've traced the gun used in Beverly Bishop's murder to her."

Nancy's heart sank. This was one time when she wasn't happy to be right. The news confirmed her worst fears.

"It was registered only the day before and

reported missing *after* the murder," the captain went on.

Nancy glanced over at Marilyn. The senator appeared even more tired and overwrought than she had the day before.

"Not only that," Captain Flynn continued, wincing, "but Marilyn's fingerprints were all over Ms. Bishop's office. They were on a threatening letter we found there, too. On top of all that, there was a shred of tape left in the Dictaphone machine with Beverly's last word on it—*kill*. Or maybe *Kil,* for Kilpatrick. Some of my colleagues have already suggested that she was trying to identify her murderer at the time she was shot."

The senator bit her lip, looking up at Nancy. "I've explained to Captain Flynn about the visit I paid Beverly late yesterday afternoon, and about the letter and how she handed it to me."

"Right," agreed Flynn. "And I believe you, Senator. But the point is, who else is going to?"

The three of them looked at one another. It was an uncomfortable moment for all of them, especially for the police captain. His instincts were up against a whole lot of evidence, and he seemed torn and uncertain.

"Look, Senator," he said finally, getting up. "You and I go back a long, long way. I know you wouldn't kill anybody, but the law is the law. I can hold off for a little while, but unless things look different in a day or two, I'm going to have to take you in."

Marilyn nodded glumly. "I understand," she murmured.

"Well, take care," Flynn remarked. "Thanks for the coffee. The next time I see you, I hope one of us has better news. In the meantime, Senator, please stick close to home and work. We'll be watching you." He added, "Sorry."

"It's all right, Captain. Thank you for coming over." The senator tried to smile, but it only made her face look sadder.

She walked Captain Flynn to the door, then came rushing back into the kitchen. "Nancy, what's been going on? What happened last night?"

"Marilyn, I'm afraid I've got some more bad news," Nancy said, collapsing into a chair. "It's Dan—he was, well, the car—there was an explosion . . ."

"Oh, no!" The senator rushed over and knelt down beside Nancy. "Is he all right?"

"I don't know, but I honestly don't see how he can be. There was an explosion, and a fireball, but I haven't been able to find out if he's all right yet."

"Tell me exactly what happened," Marilyn demanded. "From the beginning." She stood up and took a seat across the table from Nancy.

Nancy quickly recounted the events of the past eight hours, carefully leaving out some of the clues she was working on. As much as she hated to admit it, Marilyn was still a suspect and she couldn't know what Nancy had discovered, not until Nancy figured the mystery out for herself.

"How horrible!" Marilyn exclaimed when Nancy told her about the crash following the car chase.

"And Dan hasn't called or anything?" Nancy asked.

"No, he hasn't."

"I tried all the big hospitals earlier this morning, but no one had any record of him. I wonder if that means he's—"

"Let's see if there's anything about it on the news now," said Marilyn, springing up and turning on the radio. "It's possible that he escaped, isn't it?" she asked, her eyes pleading with Nancy to say yes.

"And here are the headlines at ten o'clock this beautiful morning," the newscaster announced. "There's been a coup attempt in western Guinea. The economy takes an upturn, according to the latest figures. Vietnam War hero and Congressman Matt Layton announces his candidacy today for the Senate seat now held by Marilyn Kilpatrick . . ."

Marilyn's eyes widened. "He's really going through with it," she whispered, shaking her head in resignation. "Not that I'm surprised."

"The Bullets sign their top draft, and another beautiful day on tap. More news after this—"

Marilyn turned the volume down. "That's

funny," she said. "Not a word about any explosion or car accident."

Nancy frowned. "I had a feeling there wouldn't be. When the hospitals didn't know anything and the early-morning news didn't report it, I wondered if there might not be some kind of cover-up. And if I'm right—well, anyone who can silence the press has got to be very powerful. Marilyn, I'm afraid we're up against somebody big," Nancy concluded.

"But who even knew what you were doing?" asked the senator. "I'm the only one who knows you're investigating this case," she pointed out.

"Unless your house is bugged, and your office," Nancy suggested. That would explain why someone had seemed to anticipate her every move.

"Good morning, everybody." Teresa emerged from the bedroom, yawning. "What time is it?"

"Just after ten o'clock. I canceled your morning practice session," said Marilyn. "I thought you needed the sleep more than the tennis."

Teresa smiled sleepily. "You're right about that."

Nancy found herself yawning, too. "Speaking of sleep . . ."

"My goodness, you haven't slept all night!" cried Senator Kilpatrick. "Go lie down for an hour or two, Nancy. You can't do anything if your eyes won't stay open."

Nancy nodded, standing up. "Don't let me sleep too long, though. I've still got some things to check out, and I can't waste any time."

"Just for an hour, I promise," said the senator, raising her right hand. "Come on, Teresa, let's get you some breakfast."

"Don't you have to go to work?" asked Teresa as Nancy headed to the bedroom.

"Um, not today, Teresa," answered the senator. "I've decided to take the day off."

Nancy went into the bedroom and called Pringle Press to explain that she had become sick and had had to leave. Then she crawled under the covers. Lying on her back, she felt as if the walls were closing in on her. She was torn, torn about everything. Where should she look first for the locker? Should she ask Marilyn for advice? Should she take the chapters to Captain Flynn in the hope that the investigation would shift away from the senator when the other suspects came to light? And who *was* the fourth one? Something was nagging at her, but Nancy couldn't put her finger on what it was.

Exhaustion prevailed, and soon Nancy was engulfed in a dreamlike haze. Then a sudden and terrifying scream woke her up.

Nancy sat bolt upright in bed and rubbed her eyes. Had she really heard a cry for help, or had it been part of a dream? She had to make sure Teresa was safe, even if it was a false alarm. She hopped out of bed and dashed into the living room.

Teresa was leaning against the wall, one hand over her mouth. Senator Kilpatrick was standing stock-still in the middle of the room, as if frozen.

"What's going on?" Nancy blurted out. Teresa lifted a weak finger and pointed at the front door.

There stood Dan Prosky, pale and hollow eyed. He opened his mouth and tried to speak, but only a strangled whisper came out. "He— he's dead!"

Chapter
Twelve

NANCY STOOD FOR a moment, not believing her eyes. Who was dead? And how had Dan survived the explosion?

Springing to Dan's side, Nancy and the senator guided him to the sofa and helped him to sit down. He seemed too confused to know what was happening to him.

"Teresa, please get him a glass of cold water—and some juice, too," Nancy said to her friend. "I think he's got a bad case of dehydration, not to mention exhaustion."

The senator propped pillows behind Dan's back and gently massaged his shoulders. "Just relax, Dan. You're with friends."

"I'm so sorry about what happened," Nancy said, looking into Dan's glassy eyes.

Teresa returned with two glasses, and Nancy held the water up to Dan's mouth. "Drink this, Dan. You've got to."

He raised one shaky arm and lifted the glass to his lips. Nancy was afraid he might drop it, but he managed to take a few big gulps. He sat without moving for a minute, then lifted the glass and drank again, finishing the tall glass of water.

"That's better," Nancy said. "Can you tell us what happened to you?"

"I—" Dan shook his head, trying to remember. "After I let Nancy out of the car, I drove for a couple of blocks, and then there was suddenly this—I don't know, some hole in the ground where workmen were digging, with the orange cones in front of it and all. But I was going so fast . . ." He trailed off, and Teresa handed him the glass of orange juice.

"There was an explosion," Nancy reminded him. "Was it your car?"

"No—no, I swerved just in time to miss the hole. But then the guy behind me—he wasn't so lucky. I think it must have been a gas main or something, because it was much too big a bang for just a car going up."

Nancy shivered. Maybe the car had been carrying explosives.

"And then what?" Teresa prompted.

"The blast caught my car and flipped it over. I

crawled out the window somehow and walked a couple of blocks to this little park. But then I started feeling pretty bad. I guess I must've hit my head or something, because I just lay down on a park bench and passed out for a while. I woke up with a pounding headache—I couldn't really think straight. So I wandered around for a while, until I ended up here. What time is it?" he asked.

"Eleven o'clock," Teresa answered.

"I must have been walking around for hours!"

"No wonder you look so pale," Nancy observed. "Teresa, would you call a doctor? You're lucky you made it here, Dan. You need medical attention!"

Dan sat quietly for a moment, sipping the juice. "Listen, don't you think it's time you told me what this is all about? I mean, if I'm going to be risking my neck, I should at least know what for."

"You're absolutely right, Dan." The senator nodded.

Nancy broke in. "Marilyn," she interrupted, "I've got a couple of leads to track down, so if you'll excuse me, I'll get dressed while you fill Dan in."

Nancy raced back into the bedroom to change. She was so glad that Dan was okay, but it only reminded her of the danger that lay ahead for her friends. She had to find out what Beverly Bishop kept in that mysterious locker.

Nancy pulled a sweater over her head, com-

pleting her outfit. She bent down to tie her
sneakers; she had put them on because she had a
feeling she'd be doing a lot of walking. Standing
up, she pulled the strap of her bag over her
shoulder and held the purse tightly to her with
her elbow. Inside were three chapters of Beverly
Bishop's book, still unread—and a small, blunt
key, with the number 663 inscribed on it.

"Taxi!"

Nancy's voice rose above the din of midday
traffic, mixing with the honking of horns and the
roar of engines. She could feel her energy ebbing
with every passing minute. The lack of sleep was
really beginning to affect her.

She'd had no luck at either of the city's air-
ports, and no luck at the bus or train stations,
either. She knew there must be a hundred places
with lockers in town. Nancy sighed to herself.
How would she ever find the right place?

After her last unsuccessful try, Nancy had
decided to take another tack: she'd called Jillian
Riley to see if she could meet with her. But Ms.
Riley was out of town on assignment for the day.
Then she'd phoned Della Hawks, but the maid
informed her that Mrs. Hawks was out shopping
and wouldn't be back until late.

Nancy sighed. It wasn't her day. She looked
around for the thousandth time to make sure she
wasn't being followed. All day long she'd had a
creepy feeling of being observed by unseen eyes,

tailed by unseen feet. But every time she checked, there was no one.

"Taxi!" Just when she thought she'd never get the attention of any of the speeding cabs, one pulled over for her, and she hopped in, practically crashing onto the worn vinyl of the back seat. "Fifteen twenty-five Memorial Boulevard," she told the driver, giving the senator's address. She needed sleep now, more than anything—then she'd investigate the health clubs in town. Maybe the columnist had been a member of one of them.

Nancy closed her weary eyes for a moment, or was it longer than that? She couldn't tell—she only knew that a jarring stop at a red light opened her eyes.

Nancy didn't recognize the area they were in, but Washington was a big city and she realized there were quite a few neighborhoods she had never visited. As long as the driver knew where he was going, she didn't care.

Staring sleepily out the back window, Nancy saw two hulking men, moving down the sidewalk, getting closer and closer to her.

Nancy glimpsed a familiar pair of shoes as they stepped onto the curb. A shiny pair of two-toned brown tasseled loafers was heading her way, fast. Nancy gasped. These two men had probably been following her all day, waiting for a moment when she was trapped.

Moving quickly, Nancy tossed a ten-dollar bill

onto the driver's seat, flung open the door, jumped out, and broke into a run. The shouts of her pursuers rang in her ears as the horns blared for her cab to proceed.

There was no time to look back, and no need, either. Nancy knew what was behind her—two hulks, probably armed and probably just waiting to get a clear shot at her!

Nancy sprinted into an alleyway, then onto a small street that emptied into another, and another. In this part of town, the streets were narrow and crooked, the buildings old. Unfortunately, no one seemed to work in the neighborhood, which meant that it was completely deserted at three in the afternoon on a business day. Just like the other night, there was no one to step in and save her. She was all alone, with two thugs closing on her!

With some quick maneuvering she gained a few more yards on her pursuers, turning a corner just before they rounded the last one. She ducked into a shadowy doorway for a couple of minutes to make sure they hadn't seen her, and when no footsteps sounded in the street, she stepped out and looked around.

Besides looking old, the area Nancy was in looked distinctly foreign. Signs were written in Chinese or Japanese. Then she noticed the sign on the restaurant across the street—Little Saigon, it said. Aha, thought Nancy. This was a Vietnamese neighborhood.

A phone, thought Nancy. I've got to get to a phone. Maybe Marilyn knows this area, and she can come pick me up.

There didn't seem to be any pay phones on the block, but when Nancy turned the corner she saw a familiar sign, blinking red, on and off, on and off—YMCA. Thank goodness! she thought, hurrying to the front door. There would surely be a phone in here.

Then she got a wild idea. Another thing the YMCA would have was lockers—lots of them!

Entering the building, Nancy paid the usage fee at the door and began looking around. There were no phones in sight, but Nancy wandered around the building, searching for the locker rooms. Up on the second floor, she came across a sign for the men's and women's locker rooms.

After running to the women's locker room Nancy dashed up and down the rows of lockers, searching for the 600s. But the highest number she could find was 499. If Beverly had hidden anything in this YMCA, it was in the men's locker room. Pretty smart, thought Nancy as she hurried down the hall toward it.

Pushing open the door with one hand, Nancy listened for sounds indicating someone was inside. But the gym seemed deserted on a workday afternoon, and Nancy slipped in. She kept her eyes on the lockers, hoping she wouldn't come across any towel-draped male bodies.

Nancy ran through the locker room looking for number 663. There it was! She took the key from her bag and quickly inserted it in the lock. It turned on the first try!

The door sprang open, and Nancy gasped— inside was an envelope. Was it the chapter on the fourth of the big four? She ripped it open and peeked inside.

It was a wad of hundred-dollar bills!

Nancy stuffed the envelope into her purse. She felt as if she were on a scavenger hunt!

Shutting the locker and pocketing the key, she dashed for the exit. If the thugs did find her in the locker room, she'd have no escape. And she suspected the men in the gym wouldn't be too happy to see her there, either!

The thing to do now was get back to the senator's, call Captain Flynn, and show him everything she'd managed to find. The captain was on the senator's side—he would be fair, withhold rash judgments, show consideration for her career and for Teresa's safety. It was ironic. The thugs had tried to capture her, but they'd ended up helping her find a clue.

Just as Nancy reached the door to the locker room, it swung open. She jumped behind a row of lockers. Peeking around the corner, she watched a slim Asian man of about thirty-five enter the room and look furtively around to make sure he wasn't being observed. He wore faded army fatigues over a torn blue work shirt. On his face was a terrible, disfiguring scar, as if he'd been knifed from temple to chin.

As Nancy watched, the man drew a key from his pocket and made his way down the row of lockers. He drew something from the pocket of his fatigue jacket—a cassette tape, it looked like—and bent down to open a locker.

Nancy almost cried out in surprise—the locker the man had just opened was number 663!

Chapter

Thirteen

S*LAM!*

The sound of the locker door banging echoed off the walls. The man muttered curses in a foreign language, stuffed the tape and the key back into his fatigue jacket, and stormed out of the locker room. After a moment Nancy followed him to the door, keeping a safe distance.

In his anger, the man seemed to have forgotten the secrecy of his errand. He continued to toss curses into the air, not caring who heard him, not checking to see if he was being followed.

He had intended to trade that tape for the money! Nancy realized. This man was being paid by Beverly Bishop for whatever information was

115

on that tape. It must have been very important, too, judging by the size of the payoff.

As she hurried to stay close to the man, Nancy thought back to her interview with the dead columnist. Beverly had said the information on the fourth person of the "big four" was in her head. When Nancy found out about the locker, she'd assumed Ms. Bishop had just said that to impress her, and that the real files were hidden somewhere. She had been partially right.

The truth was that even the columnist didn't know the whole story about the last of the big four. She must have arranged to buy the information from the man with the scar. The trade would take place at locker 663—the man would get a bundle of hundred-dollar bills, and Beverly Bishop would get the dirt she needed to bury someone else in scandal. Only—maybe—that someone had decided that murder was a better alternative. . . .

After a brief walk down narrow streets and around shadowy corners, the man with the scar disappeared into a doorway. A minute or two later, Nancy crossed the street and entered the same vestibule.

Looking at the names on the doorbells didn't help—she didn't even know the man's name. She ran back onto the street, crossed to the other side, and looked up at the windows, hoping to catch sight of her quarry in one of them. But no luck—most of the windows had drawn shades, or masses of plants in them, and there were no telltale movements.

After ten fruitless minutes, Nancy sighed in resignation and turned to go. Rounding the corner of the building, she noticed that there, on the street level, was the Little Saigon restaurant she'd seen before. On a sudden hunch, she went in and took a seat at the counter.

At one table sat a group of old men playing cards and drinking tea. Other tables were occupied by couples, business associates, even a family with a screaming baby and an unruly toddler. A lone waiter bustled back and forth, wiping the sweat from his brow with his sleeve, trying to keep track of all the orders.

Nancy ordered tea and a rice dish, and then scanned the room and its occupants again. A plan was forming in her head. She needed to talk to the man upstairs. If she could find him, she felt sure she could get the tape. After all, she had what *he* was looking for.

"Excuse me," she said to the waiter.

The man rushed past her shaking his head apologetically. "Sorry—very busy," he called out over his shoulder.

Nancy frowned. She had to talk to someone! The fat man sitting next to her at the counter seemed to sense her frustration. "Can I help you?" he asked, smiling. "My name is Tran," he added with a friendly nod. "What is it that you need?"

"Oh, thank you. I'm looking for a man I met last week," Nancy began, ad-libbing as convincingly as she could. "I've forgotten his name, I'm afraid. But he had a scar on his cheek, here." Nancy drew a line down her cheek with her finger. "And I'm sure he said this was his address, although he didn't mention a restaurant."

"I think you mean Louie, huh?" Tran prompted her.

"Louie, yes, that's it! Silly of me to forget, wasn't it?"

"Louie does not like people to forget his name," Tran said, waggling a finger at her and winking mischievously. "He's a pretty tough cookie! Ha, ha, ha!" He exploded in gales of laughter, drawing amused stares from some of the clientele.

"Do you know which apartment he's in?" Nancy interrupted. "I really do have to see him."

Tran's laughter ebbed, a little too quickly, Nancy thought. "You forget about Louie, miss," he advised her. "He's always with new girlfriends, so you forget him, okay?"

"No, no, it's not like that," Nancy corrected him. "It's—it's business, you see."

Tran's face darkened, and he almost looked like a different person without that broad smile. He leaned in toward her and, in a low voice, muttered, "You CIA?"

Nancy struggled not to look shocked. "Um, no,

I'm not," she said quickly. Then, taking a chance, she asked, "Is Louie?"

Tran's reaction surprised Nancy again. He broke suddenly into his biggest laugh yet and said, "Not anymore, he's not!

"So," he said, when he had finally stopped giggling. "If you are not from the CIA, where *are* you from?"

Nancy took a deep breath. "Beverly Bishop," she said, looking at Tran intently.

Tran's face betrayed nothing. He merely nodded and said, "I will go get Louie." In a flash, he was gone.

Nancy looked around her while she finished her tea and waited for Tran to return. It was amazing, she thought, how far and wide Beverly Bishop had roamed in search of scandal. And she wondered about the Vietnamese connection, too. Did the scandal, whatever it was, go back all those years to the war?

A few tense minutes later, Tran returned. He was alone and still unsmiling. After threading his way nimbly through the narrow aisles between tables, he sat back down on his stool next to Nancy. "Louie says he wants to see you. Top floor in the back. Ring bell number Five-R."

"Thank you so much, Tran," Nancy said sincerely. Leaving her check and the tip on the counter, Nancy made her way out of the restaurant and around the corner to the building entrance. Pressing 5-R, she shifted uncomfortably, wondering if she was walking into a trap. There was still time; she could leave now, call Captain Flynn, and have the police take Louie in for questioning. But when the buzzer sounded, Nancy pushed the door open and went in. She was so close to an answer—she could feel it! She *couldn't* slow down now.

Five flights of steps later, she stood in front of a gray steel door and knocked loudly three times. The door opened, and Nancy walked in.

The studio apartment was full of Vietnam War memorabilia—bayonets, medals, framed commendations from the U.S. and Vietnamese governments, and photographs covered the walls.

Louie walked over from the window and faced Nancy, arms folded across his chest. Silently he watched her as she took in the surroundings.

"I was a special agent during the war," he explained, noticing her reaction to the extensive collection of war mementos. "Undercover CIA, worked with Green Berets, SEALs, everybody."

In the dim light Nancy could just make out his chiseled features and the hideous scar that marred his otherwise handsome face.

"Vietcong cut my face," he explained, watching every movement of her eyes. One false move, and Nancy knew she was as good as dead. Louie was not a man to fool with.

"Beverly sent me," Nancy said, hoping Louie hadn't heard she was dead. She didn't see a TV in the room, which was a good sign.

"You got the money?" he asked. "Why didn't she put it in the locker?"

"It's not safe anymore," Nancy explained, hoping she sounded convincing. She felt as if she were being X-rayed by Louie's practiced eye, as if he could see right through her every lie.

Without waiting for him to respond, Nancy reached into her bag and tossed Louie the envelope of bills. He opened it and quickly counted the money, making sure every last hundred was there. When he was finished, he nodded, relaxing a little.

"Beverly's going to sell a million copies of her book with this," said Louie, reaching into his pocket and pulling out the tape. He held it up, then pretended to toss it to Nancy. She reached out to catch it, but Louie stopped at the last moment and said, "Too bad Beverly's not alive to enjoy her big success."

Nancy's blood froze. So he knew! What did Louie do to people who lied to him? She looked nervously at the assortment of weapons in the room.

"Tran tells me Beverly got killed last night," said Louie, perching himself on the arm of a chair. "He reads every paper in town, that guy. Knows everything." He smiled now, a wide, evil,

121

grisly smile almost the length of his scar. "Maybe *you* killed Beverly, huh? You got her money, right?"

"No!" Nancy said, trying to stay calm. "I didn't kill her." She decided to take a chance to see if Louie knew anything. "I'm trying to find her killer," she announced. "Do you know who did it?"

Louie burst out laughing. Shaking his head in amusement, he tossed her the tape, saying, "There's your murderer, lady. You better find him before he finds you!" And using his index finger as a gun, he pretended to shoot her. "Bang," he said softly.

So! thought Nancy. The killer is a he! She would know who he was soon enough, when she returned to the apartment and played the tape. After saying goodbye to Louie, she turned and put her hand on the doorknob.

But the door wouldn't open. Nancy tried turning the knob again, pulling, pushing—nothing worked. The door was locked from the outside. She turned and looked at Louie. "Did you lock me in here?" she accused him.

"Of course not. What would I want with you?" he said. "I have the cash." Nancy tugged at the door again; the handle felt hot in her hand. Suddenly thick black smoke started seeping into the room from underneath the door.

The place was on fire!

Chapter
Fourteen

CURSING IN VIETNAMESE, Louie barged across the room, brushed Nancy aside, and felt the door. "It's too hot. We'll die if we go out there!" he exclaimed.

Nancy covered her mouth with her handkerchief and crouched low to stay under the suffocating blanket of smoke that was quickly filling the room. "Is there another way out?" she asked, her voice muffled.

"The fire escape!" Louie shouted. Throwing the window open, he climbed out and motioned for Nancy to follow. "Come on!" he yelled, and reached back to pull her out.

Nancy looked at the old, rusted fire escape. It

didn't look as if it would hold two people, but she had no choice.

Just as she was about to grab Louie's hand and climb out of the window, a loud crack—like a gunshot—sounded from below. Louie uttered a low grunt and toppled backward, crashing against the iron railing of the fire escape. A look of surprise and bewilderment spread across his face. Nancy watched in horror as he staggered toward the open window, his hand on his chest. "He's killing me," he gasped to Nancy, his eyes wide with pain and shock. Then he went limp.

Instantly Nancy drew her head back into the smoke-filled inferno. It took every ounce of her strength to fight back the panic that was building inside her. The paint on the metal door was bubbling now as the door got red hot. The fire was just outside and creeping closer with every second!

She couldn't go out the fire escape, she realized. That was just what the killer was waiting for her to do.

There wasn't much time left. The floorboards were growing hot under Nancy's feet. Her eyes tearing and burning from the smoke, she scanned the room, frantically searching for another means of escape.

That was when the photo caught her eye. It was propped on the bureau next to the window, behind some bottles of cheap after-shave. In it, a young Louie posed brigand-style, with a bandolier of bullets crossed over his shoulders and chest and a large knife clenched between his teeth.

But what caught Nancy's attention was the other man in the picture. An American in Green Beret fatigues whom Louie had his arm around. The American was young, rugged, his face partially blurred but still recognizable. In fact, Nancy would have known him anywhere.

It was Matt Layton!

Suddenly everything was coming together. Matt Layton—a Vietnam veteran whose specialty had been undercover operations. A man who was resourceful, efficient, and remorseless—a bit of a fanatic, by all accounts. And a politician, too—one whose record was absolutely impeccable.

Or was it?

What if there had been something in Matt Layton's past—something that happened during the war in Vietnam—something that Louie knew about and was going to sell to Beverly Bishop?

Nancy remembered all the clues that pointed to Marilyn Kilpatrick. Of course! Wasn't she Matt Layton's most serious political rival? The person he hoped to replace as U.S. senator? The woman who represented everything he hated?

Matt had to be the one who'd killed Beverly Bishop. There was no other explanation. Nancy's suspicions had been correct, and now she had the tape to prove Matt Layton wasn't the hero he claimed to be.

Nancy hurriedly stuffed the tape and the photo into her already full purse. She had everything she needed now—except a way out. Nancy sat down on the windowsill. The door was useless, and stepping out onto the fire escape would surely be fatal. Other windows? That would mean a four-story drop. Nancy didn't think she could survive that.

Maybe I ought to take my chances out there, she thought, reconsidering the fire escape. When the fire fighters get here, Layton's thugs won't be able to shoot me without getting caught.

Just then, as if to prod her into action, one wall burst into bright orange flames, licking up to the ceiling. Now there was almost no oxygen left in the room. Nancy swung one leg through the window and out onto the fire escape.

Ping! A bullet whizzed past her leg and rico-cheted off the window frame. Nancy pulled her leg back inside the room, hoping to hide from the next one. Unless someone showed up soon to rescue her, she was going to die!

She glanced around the room for a phone. Hadn't *anyone* called the fire department yet? Her gaze landed on a stack of camouflage gear, piled up against what appeared to be an unused fireplace. Taking one last gulp of fresh air at the window, Nancy ran over to the fireplace and tossed the gear out of the way. She poked her head in and looked up. She could hardly believe it—a patch of blue sky!

The chimney hole was quite narrow, and Nancy knew there was a good chance she'd never make it, that she'd be stuck inside and suffocate from the smoke of the fire. But a shred of hope was better than none. Slinging the strap of her bag around her neck to free her arms, she began shinnying up the hole, coughing the whole way, and praying she wouldn't pass out before she made it to the top.

Inch by painful inch, she scratched and clawed her way up the gritty black hole that was her only chance. Below her, she could see the red reflection of the fire as it consumed the room with a great roar.

At last she managed to reach up and grab the top of the chimney. With every ounce of strength left in her, she heaved hard, pulling herself up and over onto the flat roof of the building.

Just as she made it up over the top, her purse caught on the edge and turned over. The big heavy envelope with Beverly's three chapters in it slipped out, and before Nancy could grab it, it plunged back down the chimney and into the flames!

Oh no! Nancy peered back down the hole she'd just emerged from. There, at the bottom, were the sizzling, untold secrets of Della Hawks, Jillian Riley, and Marilyn Kilpatrick.

Just for a moment, Nancy considered going

back down for them, but there was no way she could do it. By the time she got there, the chapters would be destroyed—and so would she. As she watched, the envelope turned brown, then black along the edges, and finally burst into flames.

Nancy drew back and wiped her eyes. She had to blink several times to get the ashes out, and she took a huge, deep breath of air. It smelled like smoke, but it was breathable.

Nancy checked her purse. The tape and the photo were still there, thank goodness. As evidence, it probably wouldn't be enough to convict Matt Layton, but it was certainly a good start. And now, because of a crazy quirk of fate, Marilyn's secret was safe forever, and so was Teresa Montenegro!

Nancy wasn't out of the woods yet, not by any means. The roof around her was beginning to buckle as she stood there. In just a few seconds, it would collapse, sending her plummeting back down into the raging inferno.

Nancy ran over to the side of the roof farthest from the street and looked carefully over the edge.

There was a crowd in the narrow alley below, and the fire fighters were trying in vain to get through with their trucks.

Nancy looked across to the neighboring roof. It was a good six feet away. To get there, she'd have to climb up on the roof wall and take a standing broad jump across six feet of nothingness!

There was no choice. She had to try. Steeling herself, Nancy scrambled up onto the barrier wall, keeping her weight centered low. She bent her knees and stuck her arms out behind her, ready to jump. Letting out a yell, she leapt into the air, keeping her eyes focused on the ledge in front of her.

Every muscle in her stretched forward, and she grabbed for a handhold.

There! Her hands had found a grip at the top of the opposite wall. Her nails dug frantically at the slate shingles, and her legs pumped away at the bricks. She'd made it—she'd managed to grasp the edge of the other roof! But her body was dangling dangerously beneath her, trying to pull her four stories down.

"Look! Up there!" someone below shouted, and the crowd turned its attention to her. Nancy was hanging on by her fingertips, and as the horrified crowd watched, she began to slip inch by inch.

Nancy looked down at the alley beneath her and gasped.

She was going to fall!

Chapter

Fifteen

Nancy struggled with all her might to hold on. Her ring and little fingers slipped, so she was holding on with just three fingers of each hand. They were shaking from the stress, and her middle fingers felt as if they were about to break in half.

A series of images started racing through her mind. She saw her father grieving when he heard the news of his daughter's demise. She saw Ned's face in her mind. And Bess and George—would she ever get the chance to tell all of them how much she loved them? What if the last thing she saw was the dirty red brick building she was clinging hopelessly to?

No! She refused to allow that to happen. With a grunt, she clawed at the wall, hoping against hope that somehow this wouldn't be the end.

That was when her toe found an outcropping, a tiny ledge only about three inches wide. Nancy guessed it was the stone lintel that ran across the top of the fourth-floor window. It didn't matter much what it was—it was a toehold. It would stop her fall.

She rested some of her weight on the narrow stone ledge for a moment or two while she got a more secure grip with her hands.

Breathing hard, Nancy flexed her knees slightly and took a little jump upward—about a foot's worth. Just enough to grab the inside of the retaining wall with her hands and hoist herself up—and over!

There! thought Nancy, listening to the crowd cheer. If the gunman hadn't shot her yet, he obviously wasn't going to—not with so many people around. Still, better not to take any risks with her precious evidence.

Looking around on the roof for a place to hide it, she found a pile of rubble up against one side of the water tank, the residue of a job some sloppy workmen had left unfinished. Taking her bag off her shoulder, she buried it in the pile, then covered it with debris. No one would think to look for anything under there. Her treasure would be safe until Captain Flynn could uncover it.

Now Nancy had to get down to the street and away from the thugs. Most important, she had to get home and tell the senator, Teresa, Dan—and the police!—who had really killed Beverly Bishop.

Nancy hurried over to the door to the stairs, but it was locked from the inside. Quickly she ran back to her bag, dug out her lock-picking kit, and took care of the problem in short order. She felt as though she had escaped this mess safely.

She was down the stairs and on the street in no time, shifting her gaze in all directions as she melted into the crowd on the street. Somewhere nearby lurked a couple of thugs who would just love to follow her back to the senator's home. They had killed Louie, and now they were after her. Well, she was not about to oblige them!

Every bone in her body ached, and as Nancy moved through the crowd, trying to look unobtrusive, she felt about a hundred years old. In the past twenty minutes, she'd used muscles she hadn't even known she had.

As far as was possible, Nancy kept close to knots of people, figuring that she would be a less tempting target. In this fashion, she made her way little by little down the block, toward the far corner. Around it lay safety, success—and, she hoped, no surprises.

She was about twenty yards from the corner when she ran out of people to hide behind. She lingered for a moment, undecided. Should she make a run for it or just continue to stroll until she was out of sight? If they'd already spotted her, it probably wouldn't make any difference which she did. They'd find her and catch her, no matter what. She didn't have the strength to outrun them, not anymore.

Nancy kept walking slowly, as if she were out for an afternoon stroll.

"Hey! That's her!" came a shout from behind her.

Nancy broke into a brisk run, moving as fast as she could with her aching muscles. Maybe she should have stayed in the crowd, but it was too late for that now.

Ping! A bullet ricocheted off the corner of the building as Nancy ducked around it and out of sight. No sound of gunfire, just a *ping*. The gunmen were using silencers, Nancy realized. They must have attached them to their weapons when the crowd gathered!

Nancy ran out into the street when a stream of traffic went by and tried to hail a cab, but none stopped. She ducked back into her hiding place. She was going to have to make it all the way back to Marilyn's on foot, lost and aching as she was, and with at least two goons on her tail.

Nancy felt as if she'd already spent every last ounce of energy. She'd barely slept in almost thirty-six hours, she'd been shot at, nearly burned to death, forced up a chimney and out onto a roof, and now she was being chased through the streets of Washington!

Nancy ducked under an overhang and searched the skyline for familiar landmarks. Off in the distance she could see the dome of the Capitol, and she knew where Marilyn lived in relation to that. If she could just make it to one of the big avenues, she'd be able to figure it out from there. Nancy prided herself on her excellent sense of direction—every great detective needed one.

She stepped out of the doorway and started running again at top speed. She knew she could find her way back to Memorial Boulevard. The question was, could she make it there alive?

"Marilyn?"

Nancy's hoarse voice echoed in the silent apartment. "Marilyn, are you here? Teresa?" Nancy flicked on the light, and looked around. The apartment had been straightened up, but there was no sign of Marilyn or Teresa. "Marilyn?" she called again.

"Nobody here but us congressional staffers," came a voice from behind her. With a gasp of terror, Nancy turned around and stared into the smiling face of Dan Prosky.

"Dan!" she cried out, her hand on her chest. "You scared me half to death!"

"Sorry about that." He smiled as he munched on a doughnut. "Boy, you look terrible."

"You didn't look so hot yourself the last time I saw you. Where's Marilyn? I've got to talk to her." Nancy sank onto the sofa in the living room, exhausted.

"She's at the police station."

"Oh no! Is she under arrest?"

"No, not yet. Captain Flynn said they just wanted to ask her a few questions."

"Where's Teresa?" Nancy wanted to know.

"She went along for moral support. To tell you the truth, she's probably a lot safer at the station house than she would be anywhere else."

"But, Dan, everything's all right now!" Nancy said excitedly. "Beverly's manuscript—it got destroyed, burned to a crisp!"

Dan looked at her blankly for a moment. He sat down in the club chair next to the TV. "Nancy, I was a cop for five years, you know. You could be in big trouble if you—"

"No, Dan, it was an accident. I was on my way to the station to turn those chapters over to the police. Listen, it's a long story. Right now, I have to take care of something even more important—Beverly Bishop's murderer. I know who it is, Dan!"

"You're kidding! You sure are a fast worker." Dan shook his head admiringly. "Who is it?"

"You're not going to believe this when I tell you. It's Matt Layton."

Dan just sat there for a moment, blinking his eyes. "I'm not sure I heard you right. Did you say Matt Layton, as in *Congressman* Matt Layton?"

"Mm-hm," replied Nancy. "He killed Beverly Bishop, and either he or one of his thugs killed a guy named Louie down in Little Saigon. They tried to kill me, too."

"I don't get it," said Dan, shaking his head. "The guy's a bona fide war hero. He got the Congressional Medal of Honor."

"That's just it, Dan. If there *was* something buried way back in Layton's past, and Beverly Bishop somehow found out about it—then nobody has more to lose than the guy who's got it all," she pointed out.

"I guess so," Dan agreed, scratching his head in disbelief. "But, Nancy—Matt Layton?"

"He's Marilyn's worst political enemy, right?" Nancy reminded him. "And whoever killed Beverly tried very hard to make it look as if Marilyn did it!"

"You're right," Dan said. "Do you have proof of any of this?"

"Well, I'm pretty sure I've got proof of motive for both murders. In any case, I've got enough to expose Matt Layton for whatever else he is—I haven't heard the tape Louie gave me yet, but if his information was good enough for Beverly Bishop, it'll be good enough for the rest of the Washington press corps."

"Meaning, if you can't nail him for murder, you'll settle for exposing him?"

Nancy shrugged wearily. "If I have to."

"So tell me," said Dan, crossing his legs, "where's this proof of yours?"

"In a safe hiding place," said Nancy, "waiting for the police. You know, maybe we should go down to the station and tell Captain Flynn and Marilyn what's going on."

"Okay," Dan said, standing up. "But do you want to shower that soot off first?"

"No. I'll have plenty of time to look good *after* the murderer is caught. Right now we've got to make sure he doesn't kill anyone else."

"Like you?" Dan asked as they walked to the front door.

"Exactly!" answered Nancy.

Dan reached in front of Nancy and opened the door for her. But someone was standing on the doorstep, his finger poised to ring the bell.

It was Matt Layton.

And he was pointing a revolver right in their faces.

Chapter

Sixteen

Nancy Drew, isn't it?"

Nancy stared back into Matt Layton's steel blue eyes, her heart practically in her throat. She didn't say a word.

"I'm *so* sorry it's come to this," he continued. "Really I am. Let's go inside," he said, stepping through the door and carefully closing it behind him. They walked into the living room with Layton holding a gun to Nancy's back.

"Please—sit down, both of you," he commanded. "Make yourselves comfortable."

With a questioning look at Dan, Nancy sat down on the sofa. Dan started for a chair on the opposite side of the room, but Layton stopped

138

him. "Huh-uh," he said, waving his gun as a warning. "Next to your detective friend, Mr. Prosky. That's right." He smiled at Nancy as Dan took his place next to her on the couch.

She had to admit Layton was handsome and charismatic, and he held up well under pressure. There he stood, acting as if the three of them were at a social function! The man was cool, with nerves of steel, no doubt about it. Just the kind of man you'd want to have on your side in a war.

But this *was* a kind of war, after all, thought Nancy—and Matt Layton was on the *other* side.

"My, my," said Layton, coming a little closer and looking Nancy over carefully. "You and Ms. Montenegro really do resemble each other. How unusual, for two such illustrious and unrelated people! Truly remarkable."

The initial shock of the congressman's arrival had worn off now, and Nancy began to search the room with her eyes, looking for a way out of this mess—any way at all.

"Of course you know," Layton began, "that I can't afford to let you live, either one of you. Nothing personal, although I must say you've made my life pretty miserable lately, Ms. Drew. How you managed to get out of Louie's apartment alive, I'll never know. I'm sure it's a long story, and I haven't got all that much time."

"Since we're going to die anyway," Nancy interrupted, "can't you at least tell us what it was Beverly had on you?"

Layton considered for a moment, regarding his revolver carefully before replying. "I suppose I could. Since it won't be in Beverly's book after all, and since you'll be history in a few minutes, I guess it won't hurt to tell you."

Putting one foot up on the arm of Marilyn's sofa and leaning toward Nancy, he said, "You see, Ms. Drew, Louie and I were buddies back in 'Nam, round about nineteen sixty-seven, 'sixty-eight. We were in the Green Berets together, and we did a few interesting jobs for the CIA— undercover operations here and there, counterterrorist strikes, that sort of thing. You get very close to your buddies doing that kind of work, and Louie and I, and three or four other guys—well, we did a lot of good work for the country.

"But we also had a couple of other little operations going on the side. We weren't stupid, and we knew the government wasn't going to give us the bonuses we deserved for the hard work we were doing every day. Unfortunately, the government was too busy getting itself out of debt to reward the kind of rugged individualism that made this country great."

"By 'rugged individualism,' you mean what?" Nancy challenged him. "Extortion? Theft? Treason, maybe?"

Layton didn't seem at all angered by Nancy's taunt. He merely smiled and said, "We had a contact in the quartermaster corps, and so we opened up a little business. We sold a lot of stuff—food, ammo, even weapons when we could get our hands on them. We always had lots of customers—peasants who needed to feed their families, villagers who were anxious to protect themselves from the Vietcong.

"But, of course, there was never any way of knowing *who* was going to wind up with all the stuff. As far as we knew, we were just selling it to honest townsfolk, fooling with the bookkeeping a little, and making ourselves some extra cash."

Dan sat bolt upright on the couch. "I can't believe this!" he sputtered. "Are you saying you were stealing from the U.S. government and selling goods to people who might in turn have sold them to the enemy, or who might even have *been* the enemy? That's out-and-out treason!"

"Call it whatever you want to." Layton scowled. "Dead men have the right to their own opinions."

With a wicked smirk, the congressman turned to Nancy. "Your friend is brilliant, Ms. Drew," he said. "He actually managed to put two and two together."

"He's a lot swifter than your henchmen, Mr. Layton," Nancy shot back. "They let me slip through their fingers a dozen times in the last day or two."

"Quite right." He sighed sadly. "It's almost impossible to get good help these days, as everybody knows. The guys in 'Nam were good boys.

141

Unfortunately, none of them made it back stateside—except Louie.

"But Louie didn't fare as well as I did when we got to the U.S. He was weak—he let some bad memories get the best of him, couldn't hold a job or make any real money. At first I tried to help him out by putting him on the country's payroll, but after I made it to Congress, that got a bit too risky.

"So I fired Louie from the fictional job I'd given him—paying him a nice chunk of money as severance, though, when he left. But Louie wanted more, and since he knew his information was worth a lot of money, he sold it to the highest bidder: Beverly Bishop, the reporter who'd pay thousands for a good story. Well, she paid, all right. And now—"

He stood straight, pointing the gun at Nancy again. "If you'll just be so kind as to tell me where you've put Louie's evidence against me . . ."

Nancy felt the blood rushing through her veins. The moment of truth had come. She had to delay the inevitable, in the slim hope that help would arrive or that she could find a way out.

"Come, come, Ms. Drew," Layton prompted her, gesturing around the room with his gun. "Where is it? I don't have all night. We politicians are very busy people, you know, especially when we're running for office."

"Why should I tell you?" Nancy spat out.

"You're going to kill us both, anyway, aren't you? And Marilyn's going to be arrested for murder!"

"True," Layton agreed. "But if you don't tell me—or if the tape isn't where you say it is—I might just get very angry and kill your friend Teresa, too."

Matt Layton was looking at her amusedly now, a diabolical smile lighting up his face. *How could I ever have thought he was attractive?* Nancy wondered to herself, seeing those chiseled features transformed into a mask of pure evil. *He's a monster!*

She had to stall him a little longer. "All right." She sighed, feigning defeat. "You win. The tape is on the roof of the building next to Louie's apartment. I buried it under a pile of trash. But you'll never be able to find it by yourself. Why don't I take you there and find it for you myself—"

"That won't be necessary, Ms. Drew," Layton said, waving his gun at her. "I'm an old hand at finding buried treasure. And now, if you two will be so kind as to accompany me to my car—your bodies will be discovered tomorrow morning on the banks of Rock Creek. I'm sure the police will find some way to trace your murder to Marilyn Kilpatrick."

Suddenly he froze as someone pounded loudly on the door of Marilyn's apartment. "Open up!" a voice yelled from outside. "It's the police!"

Layton spun away from his prisoners in the

143

direction of the door. That slip was all Nancy needed. She jumped off the couch and sprang at her captor, tackling Layton by the knees and bringing him to the floor.

Immediately, though, Layton recovered himself. The veteran of hundreds of hand-to-hand fights rolled Nancy over and sat on her stomach. Raising the gun over his head, he prepared to whack her on the jaw.

But Nancy was too quick. She grabbed his hand as it came down and, twisting it with all her strength, bashed it into an end table.

The gun went flying, just missing Dan's head. Dan leapt toward the foyer and quickly threw open the door for the police. With a second swift move, he scooped the revolver off the floor and aimed it at Matt Layton. "Freeze!" he yelled as Layton raised his hand for a karate death strike to Nancy's throat. The hand stopped in midair, then slowly sank, as the congressman realized the game was up.

Nancy felt weak with relief as Dan pulled Layton off her. Sitting up, she turned toward the open doorway. Captain Flynn stood there, along with at least a half-dozen police officers, their guns trained right on Layton.

"Get the cuffs on and get him out of here, Mackle," growled Flynn, stepping into the room.

"You have the right to remain silent—" Sergeant Mackle began, but Layton cut him off.

"I *know* what my rights are! And when I get my

lawyer on the phone, he'll tell you which ones you've already violated!" he threatened, glowering at the policeman.

As the sergeant snapped the cuffs on the furious Layton and continued to read him his rights, Captain Flynn helped Nancy up from the floor. "Well," he said admiringly, "looks like you two didn't even need our help."

"Oh, I wouldn't go that far, Captain," Nancy said, brushing herself off. "Say—how did you know just when to show up, anyway?"

Flynn smiled. He went over to the chandelier, reached up, and came down with a small wireless microphone in the palm of his hand. "We've had this place wired for the last thirty-six hours," he said. "The other morning when I came here to visit Senator Kilpatrick, I stuck it up there when she went to get her gun registration out of her desk. I hated to do it to an old friend like the senator, but I thought it might help us catch the murderer somehow."

He dropped the microphone into his vest pocket. "But I hardly expected a full-length confession!" he admitted, putting an arm around Nancy's shoulders.

As Sergeant Mackle pulled the congressman toward the door, Layton turned around and glared at Nancy, his steel blue eyes radiating pure hatred. "You'll pay for this!" he said between gritted teeth.

"Nancy," Captain Flynn said, an eye on

145

Layton's departing figure, "you showed intelligence, strength, moral fortitude—" He chuckled. "Maybe you ought to consider running for office someday—I hear there's a congressional vacancy in your state."

"I'll be back!" Matt Layton raved as he stumbled backward out the door, two policemen tugging him.

"I doubt it," Nancy called after him. "Not in this lifetime, anyway," she said, smiling at Dan and the captain.

Chapter

Seventeen

SECONDS AFTER MATT Layton had been whisked off in a police car, there was a commotion in the doorway. The cordon of police parted to admit Marilyn Kilpatrick and Teresa.

"Nancy! You're okay!" cried Teresa, running to her look-alike and hugging her hard.

"Thank goodness! You're alive and well! We were so worried," said Marilyn, joining in the hug. Then the senator's arm went around Nancy's shoulders, and she sighed with deep relief. "We listened to the whole conversation down at the station. I still have a chill up my spine—"

"Um, hello. I'm all right, too," said Dan Prosky, edging over to them with a little wave.

All three women cracked up simultaneously. "Oh, Dan," said Nancy with a warm smile. "You were terrific. Honestly—the best!"

"Well, don't tell them I saved *your* life," Dan warned Nancy. Turning to the others, he explained, "This girl disarmed Layton all by herself. The gun just happened to drop at my feet, that's all."

"Oh, Nancy!" Teresa's eyes brimmed over with tears. "Once again, you saved our lives!"

"How did you figure out it was Layton?" asked the senator incredulously. "The thought never entered my mind!"

"Well, I had to think fast on that one. It's pretty complicated. If you want to find out, maybe you should take us all out for a celebratory dinner," Nancy suggested with a wink.

"Absolutely!"

"Hey, what happened down at the station house?" asked Nancy, with an eye on Captain Flynn. "How did they treat you?"

The senator smiled. "Well, I did call my lawyer, if that's what you mean—" She turned toward the doorway, and there was Carson Drew standing there, attaché case in hand.

"Dad!" Nancy cried, running to embrace him. "Oh, Dad, you don't know how glad I am to see you!"

"I have a fair idea," Carson Drew replied as he watched a police officer put Matt Layton's gun in a plastic bag for evidence. "Looks as if I missed all the fun," he quipped.

"Not *all* the fun," Marilyn Kilpatrick corrected him, slipping her arm through his. "You're just in time for the best part!"

That evening Nancy, Teresa, Marilyn, Dan, Captain Flynn, and Carson Drew gathered for dinner at Dion's, the most elegant restaurant on Pennsylvania Avenue. Not surprisingly, they were eager to discuss the case that had almost cost them their lives. Nancy was glad to have taken a short nap and a shower, and to be wearing her own clothes—and hair color— again!

"But I still do not understand how they got your revolver," Teresa said. She took a sip of ice water and waited for the senator to reply.

"Well," Captain Flynn answered, "I talked with that assistant of yours—Richard."

"Yes, what about him?" the senator asked.

"He told me that before you left for the day, and as you were getting your things together, you stopped at his desk for a second. Apparently you left your bag there while you went down to check on a problem one of your speech writers was having."

"That's right, I did!"

"But why would you leave your purse somewhere when you knew there was a gun in it?" Nancy asked, surprised. "That's not like you."

"I know," admitted the senator, nodding. "But I think I was just so flustered that I didn't know *what* I was doing."

"I agree," said Dan. "You haven't even looked like yourself these past few days!"

"While Marilyn was off on another floor," the police captain continued, "Richard got a call from Congressman Layton's office—they wanted him to pick up a batch of papers at the Congressional Office Building. But when he got there, no one knew what he was talking about. And Layton's secretary had just left for the day. Richard says he waited around for a couple of minutes to see if anyone could clear up the confusion, but then he gave up and went back to his own office. On the way he passed Layton in the hall, but since Layton was often in the Senate Office Building, he thought nothing of it. It must have been then that Layton took the revolver and left the metal weight in Marilyn's purse."

"Pretty risky," Nancy's father commented.

Nancy agreed. "Matt Layton certainly has guts, I'll give him that."

Teresa frowned. "May I ask a question?"

"Go right ahead," Captain Flynn answered.

"Who put that message on the wall of my apartment?"

"That I don't know yet. My staff is doing a

thorough investigation, talking to all your neighbors, tracing the phony blood to its source. We should know in a week or so."

"I bet it was someone from San Carlos who found out about Beverly's book. I wouldn't be surprised if Matt Layton put through a person-to-person call to your enemies down there, Teresa, just to get them angry and to make all of us more nervous," submitted Nancy. She buttered a roll and took a bite.

"Confidentially, Nancy, I think you're absolutely right," Ed Flynn commented. "But until we find out for sure, I can't say anything."

"Okay," Dan said, his face screwed up in concentration, "so how did Layton know that the senator had bought a gun? Did he bug her office, her apartment, what?"

"The senator's office was bugged," Captain Flynn explained, "and one of Layton's thugs was obviously listening to the transmission night and day. He knew she had a gun, he knew when she was planning to go to Beverly's—the rest was up to him."

"I suspect that Marilyn's apartment was also being watched constantly," Nancy put in. "And whenever one of us left it, we were followed by one of Layton's men. That's how they knew to follow Dan and me to the morgue and how to trap me in that cab, and after I came home that morning just for a few minutes before going to Pringle Press, they knew I was going there, too."

"And Matt knew where to find us when he wanted to kill us, because the person who was sitting outside saw you walk in the front door!" Dan concluded.

"Speaking of Pringle Press," Nancy said, a little sheepishly, "what's going to become of Beverly's book, now that the 'big four' chapters are lost? Marilyn, did you get a chance to talk to the president?"

She smiled warmly at Nancy. "I did. Ms. Pringle isn't even interested in those final chapters—she'll just publish what she's got. But she's already signed up a hot new author—Jillian Riley's going to do a book on Beverly Bishop's murder!"

Nancy laughed. "Why doesn't that surprise me? Well, I guess it's just what you should expect in this town. I can't wait to get back to River Heights and live a normal, peaceful life."

"Normal? Peaceful?" Carson Drew protested. "I only wish you would."

"You might as well get used to it, Carson," the senator told him. "When it comes to danger or intrigue, Nancy Drew always gets elected."

Nancy's next case:

Nancy Drew and her friend Bess Marvin report to Chicago for a very stylish mystery. Fashion designer Kim Daley has been receiving anonymous death threats and has called Nancy in to investigate. But Nancy soon finds that Kim is *not* a nice person and that this case has almost too many suspects.

There's Morgan, Kim's sister and assistant, whom she treats shabbily; Paul, Kim's rejected boyfriend, who now works for the competition; Lina, Kim's most formidable business rival; and Allison, Lina's assistant. The death threats continue, but the case turns even more deadly when Nancy receives a dose of poison intended for Kim. Nancy has seventy-two hours to find the would-be killer—and the antidote—in *DEATH BY DESIGN*, Case #30 in The Nancy Drew Files™.

HAVE YOU SEEN
NANCY DREW·
LATELY?

**THE
NANCY
DREW
FILES™**

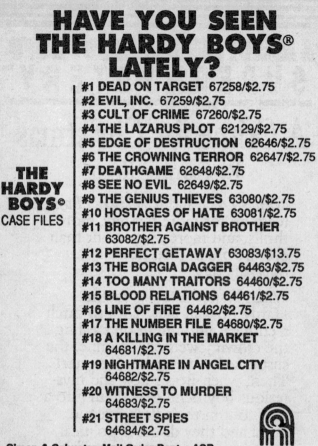